THE LATENT POWERS OF
DYLAN FONTAINE

ALSO BY APRIL LURIE

Brothers, Boyfriends & Other Criminal Minds

Dancing in the Streets of Brooklyn

THE LATENT POWERS OF
DYLAN FONTAINE

APRIL LURIE

Delacorte Press

T 9827

Published by Delacorte Press
an imprint of Random House Children's Books
a division of Random House, Inc.
New York

Delacorte Press and colophon are registered trademarks of Random House, Inc.

Visit us on the Web! www.randomhouse.com/teens

Educators and librarians, for a variety of teaching tools, visit us at
www.randomhouse.com/teachers

Library of Congress Cataloging-in-Publication Data
Lurie, April.
The latent powers of Dylan Fontaine / April Lurie.—1st ed.   p. cm.
Summary: Fifteen-year-old Dylan's friend Angie is making a film about him while he is busy trying to keep his older brother from getting caught with drugs, to deal with his mother having left the family, and to figure out how to get Angie to think of him as more than just a friend.
ISBN 978-0-385-73125-6 (trade)—ISBN 978-0-385-90153-6 (glb)
[1. Family problems—Fiction. 2. Coming of Age—Fiction. 3. Bands (Music)—Fiction. 4. Marijuana—Fiction. 5. Interpersonal relations—Fiction. 6. New York (N.Y.)—Fiction.]
I. Title.
PZ7.L97916Lat 2008   [Fic]—dc22   2007032313

The text of this book is set in 12-point Goudy.
Book design by Cathy Bobak

Printed in the United States of America
10 9 8 7 6 5 4 3 2 1
First Edition

For my sons,
Daniel and Jonny,
with love

THE LATENT POWERS OF
DYLAN FONTAINE

One

I CAN TELL YOU FROM EXPERIENCE that a jail cell is not a place you'd like to visit. Now, I'm no Papillon, and the police station serving the Sixty-eighth Precinct in Brooklyn, New York, is no Devil's Island, but it sucks just the same. To give you a mental picture, for the past thirty minutes I've been sitting on a concrete bench staring at (1) a prehistoric toilet that is no doubt infested with E. coli and gonorrhea, (2) a very large, possibly mutated cockroach snacking on a green potato chip, and (3) an entire wall devoted to words and phrases that would put even Howard Stern under the table.

I'm waiting for my father to show up and bail me out. However, the two police officers who slapped the handcuffs on me outside the Century 21 department store are having a difficult time tracking him down. My dad is a doctor—ob-gyn, to be precise—so at the moment he could be delivering a baby, performing a hysterectomy, or doing some other procedure on a woman's body, which is something I'd rather not think about. Especially after reading *Memoirs of a Pervert* on the aforementioned wall.

Outside my cell, the nice cop, Officer Burns, hangs up the phone. "Hey, Dylan, looks like your dad will be here in twenty minutes."

"Oh, okay," I say. "Thanks, thanks a lot."

The not-so-nice cop, Burns's partner, Officer Greenwood, arches an eyebrow like he's never before met such a polite juvenile delinquent, then pours himself a cup of coffee. He dumps in a buttload of creamer and stirs. I can't help myself. "Um, sir . . ." He looks up. "You might consider switching to milk or half-and-half. That stuff you just used, it's got a lot of trans fat."

He takes a gulp of his coffee and winces like he just scorched his throat. "Oh, is that so?"

I'm not being a wiseass. The truth is, for the past couple of months I've been doing our family's weekly food shopping, and I've become a little obsessed about additives, preservatives, artificial colorings, things like that. "Yeah, I read an article about it in *Newsweek*. The FDA has linked trans fats to soaring cholesterol levels. Just thought you might want to know."

He picks up the container of creamer and squints at the label. "Well," he says, "it's amazing I'm still alive." Then he rolls his eyes at Burns, who, because he's a nice guy, only smiles.

While the two of them fill out a pile of paperwork regarding yours truly, I go back to wondering what my father's reaction will be when he finds out the particulars of my arrest. I've never been in real trouble before, and since it's my seventeen-year-old brother, Randy, who's been screwing up lately, I figure I stand a pretty good chance of a lecture and a few weeks' grounding. And because my dad has other things on his mind, like the fact that my mother is now living in Greenwich Village with Philippe LeBlanc, her former art professor, he might consider the whole thing, well, trivial.

Twenty minutes later my dad walks through the door in his labor and delivery scrubs. Paper booties adorn his Nikes, and a surgical mask hangs from his neck. He sees me in the cell and rushes over. "Dylan, are you all right?"

"Yeah, Dad, I'm fine."

He looks frazzled. "I don't believe this. I thought for sure they had the wrong kid. I mean, if they'd said it was Randy, I'd understand, but . . . Dylan, what's going on?"

I hold up one hand. "There *is* an explanation, Dad. It's just, well—"

"Dr. . . . *Fontaine?*" Officer Burns stands there gaping. "Is that *you?*"

Suddenly I realize that this is my ace in the hole. My dad must have delivered Burns's baby. Maybe even saved the kid's life. My dad turns around, and when he sees Burns he shakes his head and smiles wryly. "Well, what do you know? Michael Burns. How are you? How's Christina, how's the baby?"

Burns walks over and they shake hands while Greenwood watches from a distance, sipping his poisoned coffee. "Oh, they're fine," Burns says. "In fact, we just took

Sarah in for her one-month checkup—she's already ten pounds. Here, let me show you." He reaches into his back pocket and pulls out a wallet, and when the two of them ogle baby Sarah, Officer Greenwood can't take it anymore. He picks up my stack of paperwork, raps it a few times against the desk, and clears his throat.

"Should we, uh, get down to business, gentlemen?"

Burns and my father look up. "Oh . . . yes, of course," my father says. "Sorry about that, Officer. Sorry, Dylan."

No problem, I think. *Anything to get on the good side of the law.*

Greenwood walks over, pulls a set of keys from his pocket, and unlocks my cell. The door makes a high-pitched squeak as it swings open. I shuffle out, and the four of us take seats in a nearby room. I'm not sure, but I think the place is soundproof, which makes me feel even more like a criminal.

My father takes off his surgical cap, revealing a tuft of downy blond hair. He's a pretty good-looking guy, except for the male-pattern baldness, which seems to have gotten worse with all the stress this past year. "Well, gentlemen, thankfully I'm not an expert in these matters, but shouldn't we have a lawyer present?"

Greenwood eyes Burns. Burns smiles apologetically. "Actually, Dr. Fontaine, I don't think that will be necessary. I'm quite certain we can work this out ourselves. As you were told over the phone, Dylan was caught shoplifting in Century 21, and when we searched his pockets we also found him in possession of—"

"Just a minute," my father interrupts, holding up one

hand. "Before we go any further, I'd like to know exactly what Dylan took from the store. I mean . . ." He looks at me with an expression so sad and disappointed, I want to slip under the table and crawl back to the jail cell. "You see, I give him plenty of money—actually, he earns it, mowing the lawn, cooking, cleaning. It just . . . well, doesn't make sense."

My dad is making me sound like the poster boy for *Better Homes and Gardens*, which is a little embarrassing for a fifteen-year-old guy who's six foot three and hoping to play varsity basketball this coming year. But to set things straight, he's a little mixed up about the chore list. Cleaning the house is Randy's job, which is a joke since all he does lately is lounge around the living room in the afternoons getting high with his friends. They have this rock band called the Dead Musicians Society, and cannabis, they claim, enhances their creativity. Anyway, I'm usually the one left holding the scrub brush and Ty-D-Bowl.

"And on top of that," my dad goes on, "Dylan has never really *wanted* anything before."

Now, this is most certainly true. I, Dylan Fontaine, am not a materialist. Even though I could be if I wanted to, since my dad is rich as hell.

Burns looks at Greenwood. He's too embarrassed, and also too nice of a guy, to say what I took from the store. The job goes to Greenwood. He clears his throat. "Underwear," he says, coughing a little, trying to hide a smirk that is creeping across his face. "Your son stole underwear."

My dad blinks a few times. He doesn't say anything for a

while; then his eyes widen. "You don't mean . . . ?" He looks at me, and suddenly I realize what he's thinking.

"*Men's* underwear, Dad," I say, laughing. "Don't worry, I'm not a cross-dresser."

Silence fills the room. No one thinks this is funny, and now the three of them are waiting for an explanation. I can't blame them, really. I'd be curious to know why some rich doctor's kid stole two packs of Fruit of the Loom. But right now my lips are sealed.

Later I'll tell my father the whole story—how Franz Warner, notorious drug dealer at McKinley High School, saw me shooting free throws at the schoolyard, thought I was my brother, Randy (okay, we do look alike, but obviously Franz was stoned out of his mind), and slipped me a bag of weed, which I took and stuffed into my pocket. Not that I was going to smoke it or anything, but I didn't want Randy to either. After that I hopped the bus to Century 21, grabbed two packs of tighty whities (Coach Heffner's term for briefs), got on a line with about five hundred people ahead of me, and when I was halfway to the register, thought I spotted my mother walking out the door.

At that moment I was faced with a dilemma. I really needed the underwear because our first game of the summer AAU basketball finals was taking place the following morning, and Coach said he wouldn't tolerate flimsy boxers. But I also needed to talk to my mother—apologize for acting like such a jerk on the phone the other night when she told me she was flying to Paris with Philippe for this major art show. Anyway, I quickly stuffed the packages under my shirt and ran for the door. That's when the alarm went off and a security guard grabbed me. Up until then, I'd completely forgotten about the weed in my pocket. Worst of all, the lady wasn't even my mother—just someone who looked like her.

I glance at my father, sigh deeply, and shake my head. "I'm really sorry, Dad. I needed the underwear for the big game tomorrow, and, well, the line was long and I didn't feel like waiting." At least this was partly true. I don't like to lie.

He looks at me, incredulous. "You didn't *feel* like waiting?"

I shrug. "Yeah. Sorry."

He nods slowly, pursing his lips. Meanwhile, Greenwood is getting impatient. "Dr. Fontaine, as I was saying before, we found a small bag of marijuana in your son's pocket. It's a class B misdemeanor, and I'm afraid we'll have to press charges."

My dad's eyes bore into mine. I'm not about to say anything regarding Franz Warner or Randy, not in front of Greenwood and Burns, but my dad knows I don't smoke weed and he seems to sense that there's been some kind of mix-up. "Yes, of course, I understand," my dad says. He looks at Burns. "Michael, can I, uh, have a word with you for a moment? In private?"

Greenwood is pissed about being left out. You can see the muscles in his jaw flexing. My dad and Burns leave the room, and now it's just the two of us. After a few minutes of uncomfortable silence, I say, "So . . . how long have you been in the police force?"

He gives me a hard, cold stare. "Too long, kid."

"Sounds like you don't enjoy your job very much."

He shrugs. "Does anybody?"

"Well . . ." I think about my father, who absolutely loves his job. Before my mother left us and moved in with Philippe LeBlanc, he worked sixty hours a week. Now he practically lives at the hospital. "Maybe some people do."

He offers a grunt. Needless to say, small talk is not Greenwood's forte, and soon my eyes begin to roam around the room. On the opposite wall is a bunch of framed certificates, and as I search for names and dates I discover that good old Burns was recently promoted to lieutenant. In other words, he's the Man.

Before long, Burns and my father return. Burns hands me a clear plastic bottle with a black screw-on cap. "We need a urine sample, Dylan. If it's clear, in other words if no illegal substances show up, we're going to dismiss the drug charges." He glances at Greenwood, who's still clenching his jaw and is going to have a serious case of TMJ in the morning if he doesn't stop. "Considering it's your first offense and all," Burns continues, "with no intent to distribute."

I stare at the bottle. According to Randy's friend Arthur Wellington III, aka Headbone, drinking two quarts of water per hour will flush weed from your system, consuming poppy seeds will cause a false positive for opiates, and (what most people don't know) acid cannot be detected in a piss test.

I breathe a sigh of relief. As of two weeks ago I stopped buying lemon poppy-seed muffins. They contain not only large amounts of trans fat, but also yellow #5, which supposedly lowers your sperm count.

I take the bottle and head for the bathroom. This will be easy since I've been holding it in for a while, refusing to go near the STD-infested toilet in the jail cell. When I return, I hand the bottle to Greenwood, whose job it is to perform the test. Lucky guy.

He disappears into another room, and Burns proceeds with the details. "Dylan, I'm assuming everything will go well with the sample, but you will still have to appear in court regarding the theft. There will be fines to pay, along with several hours of community service."

"Yes, sir, I understand." Personally, I think it would be less embarrassing to go to court on drug charges than for underwear theft, but I guess Burns is doing me a big favor as far as my juvenile record is concerned. "Thank you."

He holds up one hand and gives my dad and me a reassuring nod.

"So, Michael," my dad says, seemingly eager to change the subject, "tell me a little more about the baby. Is she sleeping through the night yet?"

Burns sighs, shakes his head, and while he and my dad discuss the erratic sleeping habits of baby Sarah, I begin to wonder if two weeks is long enough to flush poppy seeds from your system. But before I know it, Greenwood pokes his head out the door. "The kid's clean," he says, sounding pretty disappointed for a guy who supposedly upholds the law.

We all get up, and Burns retrieves my basketball from behind his desk. He tosses it to me and gives the paperwork to my dad. "Well, Dr. Fontaine, hopefully next time we'll meet under more pleasant circumstances."

"Oh, yes," my dad says, "you can be sure of that."

As we head for the door I see that Greenwood has poured himself another cup of coffee. This time he's drinking it black. I give him a thumbs-up sign as my dad puts one hand on my shoulder and ushers me back into the free world.

TWO

ON THE DRIVE HOME I explain to my dad how Franz Warner mistook me for Randy, and how, like an idiot, I forgot to toss out the bag of weed before entering Century 21. My dad doesn't say much, but I can tell he's pretty upset. Part of me wishes he would blow up, pound the steering wheel, scream profanities, *anything*. Instead, he sits there like a ticking time bomb.

It's close to five o'clock when we arrive home. I haven't even set down my basketball, but I can already tell from the air quality that Randy's friend Moser is here. Moser doesn't believe in bathing—something to do with his rare form of eczema—and he smells like the dead squirrel we had to fish out of our gutter last summer.

"Dyl, is that you?" Randy calls from the living room.

"Yeah, it's me." I glance at my father, who is wincing at the sound of Randy's voice. I can almost picture the acid in Dad's stomach burning a deep, festering hole.

The two of us walk in together. As usual, the whole crew is here—Randy, Nick, Moser, and Headbone. Last year, the four of them got kicked out of a high school for gifted and talented kids who supposedly think outside the box. Which is what they claimed to have been doing when they showed up for English one morning tripping on magic mushrooms. It was the beginning of Randy's demise. The guys had recently formed their band and begun dabbling in mind-altering substances.

"Dad?" Randy says, startled. "What are *you* doing home?" The rest of them sit up. Moser takes his feet off the table, and Headbone slips an empty beer bottle between two sofa cushions. It's a Heineken—my father's brand.

"Well, Randy, I *do* live here."

Randy shrugs. "Really? Could have fooled me."

My dad doesn't respond, which is probably a good thing. I wouldn't want to see him convicted on four counts of homicide carried out in his own living room. In the past, he definitely would have gone ballistic. My mother, too. After the mushroom incident my parents searched Randy's room, found his stash of weed along with a bong and some rolling papers, and after a lot of crying, tried everything to reform him—grounding, home drug tests at fifty dollars a pop, family counseling. Headbone's and Moser's parents, who had high hopes for their sons getting into Harvard, freaked out too, but Nick's folks, professors at Brooklyn College and former Woodstock attendees, chalked it up to teenage experimentation.

Anyway, all parental intervention failed, and after a

while I think my mom got tired of all the strife and scream-ing in our house. She figured it was a stage Randy was going through and it would pass. Besides, it was only marijuana. Randy swore off mushrooms due to the nasty taste and never did anything harder. My dad wasn't so keen on giving up, but when my mom left us for Philippe LeBlanc earlier this summer, that's exactly what he did.

My dad glares at Randy for a moment, then walks straight past and heads for the stairs. Except for Headbone's slight beer buzz, the rest of Randy's friends appear straight—no inappropriate giggling, no dark circles under the eyes. And then I realize—of course they're straight; the weed they were supposed to be smoking is now in the hands of my good buddy Lieutenant Burns.

Upstairs, the door of my father's bedroom slams shut. "Hey, Dyl," Randy says, "what's the deal, man, what are you doing home with the Vagina Head at five o'clock in the afternoon?" Believe it or not, Randy is not poking fun at our father. As far back as I can remember, Vagina Head has been Dad's nick-name due to his occupation.

I pluck the empty beer bottle from the sofa cushions and toss it into the trash. "I got arrested," I say. "He had to bail me out."

While Randy sits there stunned, Headbone laughs. "Awesome, dude!" He holds out one hand and, reluctantly, I do that slap-grip thing with him.

Just when I'm about to explain how the Dead Musicians Society is responsible for landing my sorry butt in jail, I hear a female voice say, "That's disgusting! Randy, how could you call your father a . . . God, I'm not even going to say it!" I crane my neck and see a girl sitting cross-legged on the floor beyond the far end of the sofa. She's holding one of my prized vintage LPs, *The Jimi Hendrix Experience*, and looks like she's about to fling it at Randy.

"Chill, Chloe," Nick says. "Randy's dad delivers babies. It's what they call those guys. He meant no harm."

She looks at Randy and narrows her eyes. "It's true, Clo," he says. "Even my mom calls him that."

I hold my breath at the mention of my mother. Randy must have slipped, because he hasn't spoken her name since she left. He hasn't even mentioned Philippe LeBlanc, who we'd been taking art lessons from and had thought was our friend. Yeah, right, some friend.

The girl, Chloe, lowers the LP and I can breathe again. At first it's hard to tell if she's pretty—her brows are deeply furrowed, her lips are pursed, and her straw-colored hair is tied up in a messy knot. But when she uncurls her face I see that she is quite beautiful—clear skin, no makeup, light brown eyes with pale lashes. She's not pretty in a conventional way, but in a way that I like. "I still think it's disgusting," she says. "*And* sexist."

Moser puts his feet back on the table. Thankfully, his shoes are on, otherwise I'd have to fumigate later. "So, Dylan," he says, tucking a few strands of long, greasy hair behind his ear, "what'd you get arrested for?"

"Shoplifting," I say without even thinking. Chloe is looking at another one of my LPs—Bruce Springsteen's *The Wild, the Innocent, & the E Street Shuffle*, and it's making me nervous. "I stole a couple of packs of underwear."

"What?" Randy says. "Are you nuts?"

"And possession of marijuana," I add. "But they dropped that charge."

Headbone starts laughing again. "Dude!"

Very slowly Randy and Nick turn to each other. From their expressions I can tell they're piecing together the events of the day. Suddenly Nick says, "Shut up, Headbone! Don't you see what's going on here?"

Headbone looks confused. "No . . . what? Ohhhh."

Now Moser gets it too. He shakes his head, and I pray to God the white stuff in his hair is dandruff and not larvae.

"Franz Warner gave you the weed, huh, Dyl?" Randy says. "Asked you to give it to me?"

"Close, Einstein," I say, "but not entirely correct. Franz Warner thought I *was* you."

Chloe looks up with a smile, which turns out to be her most amazing feature. "Ha, ha!" she says to the four of them. "Serves you guys right! Besides, you need to stay straight if you're serious about music." She tosses a pillow at Nick. It skims the top of his head and hits Randy in the face. They all laugh. I wonder which one she's in love with. Obviously, not Headbone or Moser. That's simply out of the question. My guess is Nick—he's good-looking and has what I suppose you'd call charm, but then again, so did the serpent in the garden. Randy could be the lucky one, I think, but honestly, I'm hoping it's me.

She sets down my LPs and gets up. Her clothes are unusual—loose and mismatched—and there's a tear in the knee of her jeans. She walks over to me and, on tiptoe, plants a kiss on my cheek. "Thank you, Dylan. Only, sorry you had to take the rap for these dopeheads. You didn't deserve that. I'm Chloe, by the way."

I open my mouth, but nothing comes out. I'm glad she doesn't say anything about the underwear. I can't even believe I mentioned it.

"Randy and I were in the same math class last year. That's how we met. My band broke up this summer, so the guys asked me to sing with them. We'll see how it goes. Oh, wait a minute." She goes back, picks up the LPs, and hands them to me. "These are yours. I'm sorry, I hope you don't mind that I was looking at them. I was really careful."

"Oh, no," I manage to say, still stunned by the kiss. It's the first time a girl has touched me in, well, a long time. "That's fine, really."

"Okay, okay," Nick says, obviously annoyed that Chloe is fawning over me. Well, not exactly fawning, but close. "Let's get to work, guys. Henshaw's party's next weekend and we've got a lot of songs to cover."

This is what Randy has been doing all summer—playing gigs with his friends at parties around town. Sometimes they get paid in cash, more often in pot, I suspect, but mostly they just do it hoping someone important will hear them. Someone in the music industry.

As they shuffle downstairs to the basement, where their instruments and amps are set up, I go into the kitchen, stick a sweet potato in the microwave, and pour a glass of milk, glad that there are only two ingredients in this predinner snack and I don't have to read any labels. Soon I hear Headbone warming up on drums, Moser plucking the bass, and Nick strumming his acoustic while loosening up his vocal cords.

But the one who stands out above the rest is Randy, who is on another planet musically, compared to his friends. When he picks up a guitar and begins to play, I swear, he owns it. Right now he's warming up with an awesome riff, something that must have just popped into his head. Randy used to write his own lyrics, too, but since he teamed up with the Dead Musicians Society a year ago, he's been doing nothing but covers.

Actually, that's the whole point of their band—covering dead singers. They play Hendrix, the Doors, and—since Moser is obsessed with Kurt Cobain—lots of Nirvana. Lately, though, they've been mixing it up with John Lennon, Duane Allman, and Stevie Ray Vaughan, and now, as I drain my glass of milk and pour another, I realize they've added a new singer to their list. Chloe is Janis Joplin, and she's good.

About halfway through her version of "Me and Bobby McGee," the phone rings. I swallow the last bite of sweet potato and pick up. It's the hospital, calling for my dad. One of his patients has gone into labor. It's not urgent, but the nurse is recommending a nap, since Dad may be up half the night.

I rinse my dishes in the sink, but before I go upstairs to give Dad the news, Randy opens the basement door. "Hey, Dylan, listen, I forgot to tell you. Angie stopped by this afternoon. She wants you to call." We lock eyes, and in that moment I am truly grateful that my brother is not stoned.

Besides my mom, he's the only person who understands how I feel about Angie, who, technically, is my best friend, although we haven't spoken in two months. Not since she left for her summer acting course at NYU.

Randy taps his hand against the door a few times. "You okay, man?"

"Yeah, I'm all right."

"You gonna call her?"

"No. But thanks for telling me." As he goes back to his friends in the basement, I plod up the stairs, weak-kneed, trying not to think about Angie. Right before she left, I told her exactly what I thought of her asinine boyfriend, Jonathan Reed—a junior on the debate team who thinks he's all that because he reads Jack Kerouac and James Joyce. But the truth is I wanted to be more than just a friend to Angie, only I was too much of a coward to tell her.

I look around for my dad—in his bedroom, in the bathroom, in his study—but I can't find him anywhere. Maybe he's already left for the hospital. It wouldn't surprise me.

I'm not feeling well, so I go to my room and lie down. Later, when the guys leave, when things are quiet, I'll take out *my* guitar—a handmade classical beauty from Spain with a body of pure cocobolo rosewood. My friend Jake, who's the starting point guard on our basketball team, is the one who got me hooked on classical guitar. Before that I used to play rock and blues on electric, just like Randy—he's the one who taught me—but when you have a brother who's a musical genius it's kind of hard to measure up. So, instead of trying, I chose a different path.

After a while I hear Tripod meowing. *Stupid cat.* He probably got locked in some closet and is now frantic to get out and use the kitty litter. Since I'm the one who would have to clean up the mess, I go into the hall and listen carefully. The noise seems to be coming from my mother's studio, which is really weird because as far as I know, none of us have gone in there since she left.

I push the door open. My dad is sitting in a chair, staring at a half-finished self-portrait my mother started over spring break. It's a pastel with a lot of purple, green, and yellow—colors that will eventually be blended to form the contours of her face, neck, and shoulders. That is, if she ever comes back.

Tripod is sitting on my dad's lap, and surprisingly, my dad is petting him. He's always hated that cat—a scraggly, half-feral tabby with three legs and a stump for a tail. My mother rescued him from a boatyard in Sheepshead Bay a few winters ago. She wanted to take him with her when she left, but Philippe LeBlanc's landlord has strict rules about pets.

I pull up a chair and sit next to my father. His eyes never leave the pastel. Tripod looks at me, meowing angrily, and I don't have to be Dr. Dolittle to understand what he's saying. My mother has abandoned him, too.

"Dad?"

"Hmm?" He looks my way, but his eyes are glassy and unfocused. Suddenly Tripod sees the open door, digs his claws into my dad's thigh, and bolts. "Damn, *stupid* cat," Dad says.

"Are you . . . okay?" I ask.

"Yeah," he says, "I'm fine."

"Well, I just wanted to tell you, one of your patients went into labor. A nurse from the hospital called. She suggested you take a nap."

He smiles a little. "Oh, did she now?" The reason this is funny is because we all know that if one of his patients is in labor, he's right there, by her side, the entire time. That's the kind of doctor he is.

He's about to get up from the chair, but I stop him. "Dad, wait, please. I want to explain why I ran out of the store today, you know, with the underwear."

"Oh?" He cocks his head. "You mean there's more to the story?"

I nod. "I thought I saw Mom walking out the door so I ran after her. Only, of course, it was someone else."

My dad doesn't say anything, and suddenly I can feel the emptiness in every corner of the room. Her room. He places a hand on my shoulder and his Adam's apple slides up and down. It's one of those rare male bonding moments between my dad and me, which, frankly, I find embarrassing. Finally, he says, "Dylan, as you know, I'm not exactly . . . *thrilled* about what happened today. But honestly, you're such a good kid and, well"—he looks around the room—"you don't deserve this."

What my dad means is that I don't deserve to be motherless, but as usual he dances around the subject. The funny thing is we've never actually spoken about *why* my mother left. I guess the whole Philippe deal is too painful and humiliating for my dad. But I know he misses her. I *know* he does. "But Dad," I say, "neither do you."

He holds up a hand to stop me, shaking his head like he knows better. "Believe me, Dylan, I've made plenty of mistakes. Plenty." I wonder if he means working 24/7, not spending any time with my mom when she *was* home, not taking an interest in her art or her artist friends, which is what they used to fight about all the time. At least I don't have to listen to them yelling anymore.

From the basement I hear Randy break out into an amazing lead on Jimi Hendrix's "All Along the Watchtower." He's even got the feedback going, which is no easy thing. "Listen," my dad says, "you know I don't like to draw comparisons between you and Randy, but please, do me one favor, all right? Be true to yourself. Don't . . ." He hesitates and finally decides not to finish the sentence. But I know what he was going to say. *Don't wind up like your brother.*

He pats my shoulder a few times, and as he gets up and walks out the door, Randy wails on his guitar. I smile sadly. *Don't worry, Dad, even if I tried I'd never be like Randy.*

Three

OUR FIRST GAME of the AAU summer basketball finals is scheduled for nine o'clock the following morning, and when my alarm goes off at seven, I open my eyes and see Chloe. She's sitting on the floor about three feet from my bed with a new stack of my prized vintage LPs on her lap. "Hey," she says, as if girls appear in my bedroom in the wee hours on a routine basis, "hope you don't mind. I couldn't sleep."

Sleep? She slept here? I sit up, dazed, hugging the sheets to my chest. I've been lifting weights all summer, but I'm still pretty skinny and a little self-conscious about my body. Especially around girls.

Chloe, on the other hand, doesn't seem the least bit concerned about my lack of clothing. Or hers. As my eyes begin to focus I see she's got on a pair of Randy's old boxers along with this silky sleeveless top; no bra. I'm not an expert, but I do glance at my mom's Victoria's Secret catalog every now and then, and I believe what Chloe's wearing is called a camisole. Her hair, I notice, has been unleashed from that messy knot and it pours over her shoulders in golden waves. Smiling, she holds up my 1977 *Saturday Night Fever* LP. "This is *so* cool! Can I play it?"

"Um . . ." The truth is, I rarely play my LPs, since they're collector's items and scratches lower their value. Also, it's seven o'clock in the morning and if my dad had a delivery last night, he might be in bed right now trying to catch a few winks. But seeing that I'll probably never sell my LPs, and since Chloe is very eager to hear some old disco tunes, I shrug and say, "Well, all right." I'm wearing boxers, but the problem now is how to put on a shirt without her seeing my scrawny chest. I point across the room. "The, uh, turntable is right over there."

"Oh, okay, great." She gets up and starts fiddling with the dials while I open my dresser drawer and grab the first thing I get my hands on. Thankfully, it's my CBGB T-shirt—the one Angie bought me last Christmas when we went tooling around the Village like tourists. They closed down the music venue a couple of years ago, but there's still a gift shop where you can purchase memorabilia. I figure this article of clothing will impress Chloe more than my SpongeBob SquarePants shirt.

"Here, I'll help you with that," I say. Unlike my upper body, my legs are fairly developed, so in an effort to appear cool with this whole girl-in-the-bedroom scene, I forgo the jeans.

"Nice shirt," she says as I place the needle in the groove

of "Staying Alive" by the Bee Gees—which is what I'm trying to do as her bare arm brushes against mine.

"Oh, thanks." I turn the volume low, hoping no one in the house will wake up, come into my room, and spoil the moment.

Meanwhile, she tosses the *Saturday Night Fever* jacket back onto the pile and grabs the Rolling Stones' *Sticky Fingers*. I keep this LP separate from the others because on the cover is an old Andy Warhol photo of a guy's rather large jean-clad crotch. It's got a real brass zipper attached, and it won't lie flat. Chloe plops onto my bed and very carefully slides down the zipper. "You know, I always forget what CBGB stands for."

"Country, bluegrass, blues," I say, pointing to the first string of letters on my chest, trying not to think about the fact that a girl in a camisole is sitting on my bed playing with a guy's zipper. "And Other Music for Uplifting Gormandizers," I add, sliding one finger beneath the letters OMFUG.

She purses her lips. "And . . . what exactly *is* a gormandizer?"

"A voracious eater," I say. "In this case, of music." Chloe nods, obviously impressed with my vocabulary, and I'm feeling pretty good about my level of cool. "So, you, uh, slept here last night?"

Slowly she pulls the zipper up and down, smiling the whole time. I'm pretty sure she knows what she's doing, and as far as I can tell she's enjoying it. "Remember?" she says. "I told you, I couldn't sleep."

"Oh, right."

"But I did stay here, in case you're wondering. We all did. Our band is practicing today. Next week, when school starts, we won't have much time."

At the mention of school I suddenly realize why I woke up at this god-awful hour. Our first game of the finals is at McKinley High. Also, I have to stop by my buddy Jake's house first for a pair of tighty whities. "Yeah, I heard you singing yesterday. It sounded really good."

"Thanks."

"But, uh, listen, I kind of need to get ready now."

Chloe shrugs. "Okay." At this point I expect her to leave and give me a little privacy, but she just sits there tapping her toes to "Disco Inferno." I sigh, grab my uniform from the closet, and trek out to the bathroom. On the way, I notice that the guest room door is slightly ajar, so I peek inside. As a blast of noxious air hits me, I see Moser curled up in bed, making an oil slick on my grandmother's favorite goose-down pillow. On the floor beside him is Headbone, sprawled out on the futon my parents brought home from Japan last year. He's drooling on the cherry blossom design and snoring like a bear.

Suddenly Nick appears in the hallway, shirtless, a pair of faded jeans hanging low on his hips. Unlike mine, his recent interest in weightlifting has paid off. He yawns and stretches. "Hey, Dyl, you see Chloe anywhere?"

"Yeah," I say, "she's in my bedroom."

His eyebrows shoot up, and I walk past him grinning like an idiot. In the bathroom I get changed, and after brushing my teeth and splashing cold water on my face, I tiptoe out into the hallway and take a quick look in Randy's room. He's sound asleep, no traces of a girl having spent the night. Next I turn the corner and scope out the game room. On the pull-out sofa bed, among a tangle of sheets, I see Nick's Florida State T-shirt lying next to a black lace bra.

I hear giggles coming from my room now, but I don't go back, even though I've forgotten my wristbands—a very important part of your basketball uniform if you sweat a lot, which I do. Instead, I go downstairs to the kitchen, take out the blender, and whip up a soy protein shake, turning the dial to "liquefy." Since Nick and Chloe are having such a grand old time in my room, I don't care if the whole house wakes up.

A few minutes later, Chloe strolls into the kitchen with Nick tagging behind. I stand at the counter downing my shake while Chloe takes a seat at the table and Nick opens the pantry. I haven't gone food shopping in a while, so there's not much to choose from. He shuffles around for a few minutes and finally says, "Hey, Dyl, have you bought any of those Pop-Tarts lately?"

I feel like saying to him, *Do I look like your houseboy?* But I don't. Instead I say, "No, dude, too much trans fat." I'm not really sure if this is true, since I haven't checked any Pop-Tart labels, but I figure there has to be some kind of carcinogen in the neon-pink and blue frosting.

"What?" He sticks his head farther in, shoving a bunch of cereal boxes to one side.

"Trans fat," Chloe calls. "Dylan's right, Nick. You shouldn't eat that crap."

He pokes his head out. "Oh, really? Says who?"

She rolls her eyes. "Says everyone."

With a grin on his face, Nick abandons his search, bolts to the table, and wraps both arms around Chloe. "Well, you know what, Clo? I happen to like Pop-Tarts, and I don't plan on living long enough to be some old geezer worrying about trans fat." He bends over and nuzzles her neck, and I swear I want to punch the living daylights out of him.

"Cut it out!" she says. "Get off me!" But even with her protests, she seems to be enjoying it. Which reinforces my belief that I will never understand girls.

As I down the last of my shake, Nick lifts the edges of Chloe's camisole and tickles her. She swats his hands away, but he continues undaunted. That's when I see Randy standing in the doorway. He watches for a few seconds as the two of them laugh hysterically, and I can tell he's pissed. But when it comes to Nick, or any other member of the band, for that matter, Randy is loyal. Once, when Headbone was stoned and spilling his guts, he let it slip that the members of the Dead Musicians Society had taken a vow to never let anything or anyone get between them. No parents, no brothers, and especially no girls.

Before Nick and Chloe have a chance to see Randy, he walks off in the direction of his room. Quickly, I rinse out the blender, jog to the pull-out sofa, grab Nick's shirt lying beside Chloe's bra, and toss it into the guest room, where Moser and Headbone are still snoring away in a cloud of stench. No need for Randy to know every last ugly detail of the previous night.

I've got to hurry now, so I grab the wristbands from my

room, phone Jake to ask him to bring the underwear to the game, and run out the front door. That's when I smell the sickly-sweet aroma of burning weed. I stop in my tracks and look up to the balcony—the one that leads to my parents' bedroom and overlooks the Verrazano Bridge. Randy is sitting in a lounge chair, staring across the water. It's seven-thirty in the morning and he's already smoking a joint. From this I gather three things: (1) Franz Warner makes late-night deliveries, (2) my father never made it home from the hospital, and (3) Randy is hopelessly in love with Chloe.

Our team, the Shore Road Titans, loses to the Bay Ridge Bulls by two points, and while Jake and the guys are commiserating over our loss, I'm not even thinking about basketball. I say goodbye to the team, hop the bus, and head to Ramone's—this ratty music store on Third Avenue where I buy some of my old LPs. I go to the J section, search for Janis Joplin, and bingo, there she is—*Greatest Hits,* circa 1973. The LP is twenty-five dollars and not in the greatest shape, but I don't care. I buy it anyway.

When I get home, I hear Randy and his band practicing in the basement. They're doing Moser's favorite—Kurt Cobain's "Smells Like Teen Spirit." Usually the guys joke around and call the song "Smells Like Moser's Armpit," but when I go downstairs I take a deep breath and realize Moser has bathed. Washed his hair and everything.

Chloe, who is singing backup and playing a wicked keyboard, sees my surprised expression. When they finish she says, "Yes, Dylan, it's true, a miracle has happened today, and you can thank *me* for it."

The rest of the guys, minus Moser, begin to cheer. In mock tribute, Headbone falls on his knees and bows before Chloe. She laughs and says, "We dragged Moser into the shower this morning. It took twenty minutes before the water ran clear."

"Yeah, and my eczema is already starting to flare up," Moser says, plucking his bass and giving his neck a good scratch.

"Oh, poor baby," Nick says. "Maybe we should sprinkle some talcum powder on you."

Headbone pops up. "Dude, want me to pin him down?"

I smile at Chloe. Not only is she beautiful and multi-talented, but she has also greatly improved the air quality of our home. "Oh, this is for you," I say, holding out the LP.

She looks at it and blinks a few times. "Dylan, that's so sweet. Thank you."

I drink in the moment, but then I picture Randy's face in the kitchen doorway this morning, and I remember why I bought the LP. "Actually, it wasn't my idea," I say. "Randy asked me to pick it up for you." I dig into my pocket and pull out a five. "Here's the change, bro."

He gives me a long, hard stare before accepting the money.

"Randy!" she says. "God, you're full of surprises, aren't you?" She walks over and plants a kiss on his cheek.

"You can use my turntable," I say, "you know, in my, uh, *bedroom*, anytime."

Nick rolls his eyes.

"Thank you, Dylan," Chloe says, scanning the list of songs on the jacket.

Now Randy is shaking his head and grinning at me. As the band warms up for its next song, I practically float up to the kitchen—until the music stops and Chloe calls my name. "Oh, Dylan, wait!"

I turn around.

"There's a girl upstairs waiting for you. Said her name's Angie."

Four

VERY SLOWLY, I climb the second flight of stairs and enter my room. Angie is sitting on my bed, back against the wall, shuffling through a stack of photos. Right away I see they're the ones of her and me—a collection I put together over the summer, dating back to when we were in sixth grade. Normally, when I'm not looking at them, they're in my desk, shoved way in the back, so no one will accidentally discover how hopeless I am. So much for that.

"Dylan?" she says, setting the pictures aside, not even trying to hide the fact that she's been snooping around my room. "Why haven't you called? Didn't Randy tell you I stopped by yesterday?" Angie looks the same, only better— long, straight copper hair, scrutinizing green eyes, freckles on every part of her body. Well, at least all the parts *I've* seen. I can't speak for her main man, Jonathan.

"Yeah, Randy told me," I say with a shrug. "But I've been

kind of busy." She's barefoot, wearing a lavender tank top and black Adidas running shorts. I try not to look at her legs, long and toned, stretched out and crossed at the ankles. "Besides," I add, "I could say the same to you. Unless, of course, they don't have phones at NYU."

She sighs. "Look, Dylan, you *know* why I didn't call this summer." Before Angie left for her acting course at NYU, she made it clear that I needed to apologize for dissing her stupid boyfriend. But as you can see, I did not cave in.

I widen my eyes in mock bewilderment. "No, really, I have no idea. Please, enlighten me."

Angie hates when I'm a wiseass. Which I am, a lot of the time, especially around Jonathan when he's quoting Nietzsche and Kafka. She narrows her eyes and for the next few minutes we have a staring contest. It's what we used to do when we were younger—see who could hold out the longest. Angie's good, but I'm better, and now as I expertly flare my nostrils, curl my upper lip, and wiggle both ears, Angie cracks a smile. "You idiot!" she yells. And before I can duck, she flings a pillow, grazing the side of my head. "Jonathan and I broke up. Okay? Are you happy now?"

At first I'm not sure if I've heard right, since my ear is still ringing from the blow. I walk a little closer to the bed. "Did you just say . . . ?" I'm afraid to speak the words, afraid saying them aloud might break the spell.

She nods.

It's a miracle. For the past few months I've been dreaming up ways to rid the earth of Jonathan Reed—drive him off a cliff, poison him slowly with antifreeze, serve him shish kebab on a stick of lethal oleander. Now, in one second's time, I feel like I'm about to fly. "When did this happen?"

She shrugs. "About a week ago."

"I guess you figured it out then?"

She looks puzzled. "You mean . . . you knew?"

"That he's a pretentious, condescending jackass? Of course."

She rolls her eyes. "No, that's not what I meant. Did you know he was seeing Hannah Jaworski?"

This comes as quite a shock. Hannah Jaworski is this untouchable senior with a 4.0 GPA and the body of a goddess. "No, I didn't," I say, and suddenly I really do feel sorry for Angie. She's never handled rejection well.

I sit down beside her, resisting the urge to play connect-the-dots with the freckles on her knee. "I'm sorry," I say. "Really."

She hangs her head. "Thanks." We sit there together, not saying anything, and after a while Angie picks up the photos. "I . . . found these in your desk. I hope you don't mind."

I shake my head. "Nah, it's okay."

She pulls one from the stack and smiles. "This is my absolute favorite. God, remember that day?"

It's kind of funny, because the picture she's chosen is my favorite too—Angie and me standing outside this sleazy West Side flea market in Manhattan. She's holding our purchase—a small glass fishbowl—and inside the bowl, swimming in a sea of Ozarka water, is our new pet goldfish, Tony. Earlier that afternoon I'd won him at the Feast of San

Gennaro in Little Italy, but his plastic bag had sprung a leak and we'd had to find him a new home, pronto. "How could I forget?" I say. "We had a blast that day."

"Yeah," Angie says. "But poor Tony."

I nod sadly in agreement. We had decided to keep Tony at my house, but after a few days Tripod (mangy killer that he is) got his paws on him. We buried Tony's chewed-up remains in my backyard and had a small funeral service. Even Randy and his friends attended. Afterward, Headbone suggested an execution for Tripod, death by hanging, which I thought was a pretty good idea, but Angie said no, there'd been enough bloodshed that day.

"So," I say, hoping Angie will now fall to her knees and declare her undying lust for me, "why . . . exactly, are you here?"

"Why do you think?"

I bounce a few times and pat the mattress. "I don't know. Sex?"

She groans, grabs another pillow, and hits me over the head. "I'm here, Dylan Fontaine, because you're my best friend."

Alas, the friend thing again. My lot in life, it seems.

"*And* I have a favor to ask," she adds.

"Hmm, I should have known there was a catch. What is it this time?"

"Hold on," she says, "I'll show you." She hops off the bed and retrieves a black canvas bag from behind the door. Gingerly, she pulls out a very expensive-looking video camera and smiles. "It's digital," she says. "A Sony HC3. I'm going to shoot a movie."

"A movie?"

"Yes, a short, which, in case you don't know, means a short film." She plops down on the bed again and hands me the camera. It's got a lot of gizmos. Like mine, Angie's parents are loaded, so price tags are never an issue.

I'm about to ask what the favor is, but she goes on about the camera. "Isn't it cool? And when I get enough footage, I can edit on my iMac. I've got the software to add sound, background music, subtitles, anything I want."

I study the camera without a clue as to which button does what. "Pretty fancy," I say, "but—"

"And there's going to be a screening for the summer students at NYU right before Thanksgiving. They're planning to give awards to the top three films."

I look at her, puzzled. "Wait a minute. I thought you took an *acting* class at NYU."

"I did," she says with a shrug, "but I also sat in on this awesome filmmaking class and discovered that's what I *really* want to do. Create my own movie, start to finish. The professor said I could participate in the screening."

"Hmm, interesting. Okay, so what's the favor?"

She grins sheepishly. "I need a partner, someone to give me advice, bounce ideas off of. I can't really do it alone."

"I see." Slowly I hand her back the camera.

She bites her lip. I'll admit, in the past Angie has had me wrapped around her finger, but I've learned a few things about girls since then—like how coy and fickle they can be—and now I like being in control. "So . . . Dylan," she says, somewhat nervously, "what do you think?"

What I think is that I'm not her first choice. The odds

are, before Angie found out about Jonathan dating Hannah Jaworski, she was planning to ask *him* for help, since Jonathan is no doubt an expert screenwriter and cinematographer or whatever you call those guys. "I'm not sure," I say, stringing her along. "What's the movie about?"

She fiddles with the controls. "I don't *exactly* know yet."

"Wow, sounds like you've got quite the plan."

Playfully she sticks out her tongue, turns on the flash, and takes a close-up shot of my face. Big orange splotches dance before my eyes. "Gee, thanks," I say.

"You're welcome. Actually, Dylan, I do know *one* thing about the movie. I'll be shooting it in Washington Square Park. I spent a lot of time there this summer, since my dorm was just a few blocks away. It's the perfect spot."

It figures. Of all the places in New York City, Angie picks the one with the most crazies per capita. Also, if I remember correctly, the park is not too far from Philippe LeBlanc's fancy Greenwich Village apartment, which makes me a little uneasy. Angie doesn't know yet about my mother moving in with Philippe or their recent trip to Paris—she left for NYU before it all happened. "Washington Square Park?" I say. "Are you sure?"

"Oh, yeah, definitely. And I think the film is going to be a documentary, or maybe something a little more avant-garde. I'll need to experiment, but I thought we'd begin interviewing some of the locals and go from there. Ideas will flow. At least, that's what our professor says."

I give Angie a skeptical look. Even though Washington Square Park is near some pretty high-priced real estate, on any given day you'll find your quota of chess hustlers, weirdos, and guys you wouldn't like to meet in a back alley. "Oh, and you expect these people at the park to cooperate? To bare their souls to some nosy redheaded girl wielding a very expensive camera?"

She shrugs. "Well, yeah. Why not? And besides, you'll be there. I mean, who's going to mess with me when I've got a six-foot-three bodyguard?"

I can't help it; I crack a smile. "I have been lifting weights this summer," I say, rolling up my sleeve and flexing my bicep. "Did you notice?"

"Hmm." She reaches out like she's going to pluck a miniature chocolate from a box and gives my muscle a squeeze. "Not bad, Hercules," she says. "Now, what do you say, will you do it? Will you help me?"

And just like that, we're back at square one. I'm Angie's slave again. "All right, fine, whatever," I say. "I'll help you with the film."

A big smile spreads across her face. "Thanks, Dylan." She leans over and tugs the corner of my basketball jersey. "Now, come on, hit the showers, we've got a lot of work to do."

When I emerge from the steamy bathroom, towel around my waist, I hear the Dead Musicians Society doing "Piece of My Heart," and Chloe's husky voice floating up the stairs. Angie's no longer in my room, so I figure she's in the basement listening to the band play. I get dressed, but just as I'm about to join them I notice that the door of my mother's studio is ajar. I peek inside and see Angie standing at the far end near the picture window. "Hey," I say, "whatcha doing?"

"Oh, just . . . wandering."

I walk in and stand beside her. She's gazing at a collection of sketches taped to the wall. Most of them are my mom's and Randy's creations, but a few are mine. As soon as Randy and I were old enough to hold a stick of charcoal, my mother had us drawing, and just like with our musical abilities, Randy's artistic talents have always surpassed mine. Angie knows this too, but she doesn't compare. "So," I say, "which one's your favorite?"

She points to a graphite sketch I did last year—a still life featuring a half-empty wine bottle, an avocado, and a wedge of Swiss cheese. Boring, I know, but it did win an honorable mention in the Kings County high school art show. "Of yours," she says, "I've always liked this one."

"Hmm." I study the drawing. The shadows are good, and technically it's sound, but next to Randy's portraits and gesture studies it lacks something—life, emotion, originality, all of the above.

"Have you been drawing this summer?" Angie asks.

I think about the summer art project I've been working on, due the first day of school—an old master sketch of a da Vinci drapery—but decide not to mention it. The sketch is full of detail, which is what I'm best at, but Angie tells me if I am going to be an artist I need to branch out, take chances, put myself on the line. I guess that's what she admired so much about Jonathan—not that he's an artist, but according to Angie he's a freethinker, willing to take on new ideas. New girls, too, it seems. "Yeah, I've been sketching some," I say.

Angie runs her fingers along the edges of my drawing, then takes a seat beside the easel where my dad and I had our recent father-son bonding moment. While she gazes at my mother's half-finished pastel, Chloe belts out, *"Take it! Take another little piece of my heart now, baby!"*

"She's good," Angie says.

"Yeah, Chloe is their new Janis Joplin. She plays keyboards, too. Oh, and she got Moser to shower. Can you believe it? He even washed his hair."

Angie laughs. "No, that's not what I meant. Sure, Chloe sounds great, and thank *God* about Moser, but I was talking about your mother. This pastel she's working on, it's . . . well, beautiful."

"Oh . . . yeah, I guess it is." I swallow and a strange silence fills the room.

"Dylan?" Angie says. "Where *is* your mom?"

The million-dollar question. I take a deep breath, pull up a chair, and sit beside Angie. As I struggle for words, Tripod jumps into my lap. I want to swat his mangy behind, but instead I pet him a few times. "My mother is . . . well . . . she's gone."

"*Gone?* What do you mean?"

"She left," I say. "Moved in with that guy, her old art professor, Philippe LeBlanc."

"But . . . ," Angie says. "I don't understand. Why?"

I give her a look like *Must I really spell it out?*

"Dylan, you can't mean she's having an affair? I thought you said . . ."

It's kind of ironic, because Randy and I used to joke around and call Philippe LeBlanc Philippe the Fag, since he fit the whole clog-wearing, purse-toting gay artiste stereotype. At the time it was kind of funny. Not anymore.

"Yeah," I say. "I guess we all thought Philippe was gay. But apparently not. Anyway, he and my mom are in Paris right now. They have a show together."

"Oh, God." Angie reaches for my hand, and I let her take it; in fact, it suddenly feels like I'm holding on for dear life. "I'm so sorry, Dylan. I had no idea. What about your dad? How's he taking it?"

"I don't know, really. We don't talk much, since he basically camps out at the hospital." I look into Angie's eyes, and before I know it I'm spilling my guts. I tell her about getting arrested with underwear shoved up my shirt, about the Franz Warner drug deal gone awry and the piss test performed by Officer Greenwood.

"Unbelievable," she says. "Man, you sure got the bum rap."

"Yeah, tell me about it. I've got to go to court next week too, and there'll be some hours of community service. But at least the drug thing isn't on my record."

"What did Randy say? I hope he apologized."

I shake my head. "No, but he *did* manage to hook up with Franz Warner in the middle of the night. When I left for the game this morning, he was outside smoking weed on my parents' balcony."

Angie studies me for a while. "You're worried about Randy, aren't you?"

"Um, mostly I want to kill him, but yeah, I'm worried. Since my mom left, he's been getting high with his friends every day."

Angie sighs, shoos Tripod off my lap, and leads me back to my room. We sit on the bed and she gives me a hug. Man, it feels good. I'm not even thinking about sex right now; all I know is that my best friend is back.

Suddenly I hear a loud "Ahem!" and when I look up I see every member of the Dead Musicians Society—Moser, Headbone, Randy, Nick, and Chloe—standing in the doorway grinning at the two of us.

"Well, hello *again*, stranger," Randy says to Angie. "Looks like you and Dyl finally hooked up, huh?"

Angie smiles, keeping one arm around my waist. "Hey, Randy, hey, guys."

Moser scratches his neck, which is beginning to resemble a stalk of strawberry rhubarb. "You, uh, enjoying yourself there, Dyl?"

"You know it, dude. Keep showering and one day this may even happen to you."

Everyone laughs, except Moser. "Hey, come on, guys, you know I have a problem!"

Nick swaggers in and takes a seat atop my dresser; the rest of them follow. "Welcome back, Angie," he says, and right away I can tell what's going through his devious mind. Now that Angie's home, it's one less guy to get between him and Chloe. We'll see about that.

Meanwhile, Chloe has put on my *Sticky Fingers* LP, and surprisingly, I don't even freak out about scratches and depreciation. As "Brown Sugar" begins to play, she gives Angie one of those mysterious girl smiles. "So, I thought you and Dylan were just friends," she says. I'm not sure, but I think Chloe might be jealous.

"Yep," Angie says, tousling my hair. "We are. Best friends."

And then Headbone, who looks likes he's been smoking some pretty strong reefer, elbows Moser and whispers something in his ear, and the two of them charge toward the bed, yelling, "Upset the fruit basket!" Like maniacs, they hop on and begin bouncing us around until my head rattles.

Angie grabs the pillow she smacked me with and flails it at the two of them. That's when I see Nick and Chloe in the corner of the room, dancing to my LP. His hands are moving up and down her hips. I glance at Randy leaning against the opposite wall watching the two of them, and suddenly I know what I have to do. I walk over to Nick, tap him on the shoulder like those guys in the old movies, and say to Chloe, "Excuse me, but may I have this dance?"

Chloe doesn't even hesitate. She ditches Nick, and while he stands there, jaw flapping, I take her in my arms. We dance for a while, looking into each other's eyes, and the next time Mick wails out "Brown sugar!" I do this amazing deep lunge tango move and kiss Chloe right on the lips.

Headbone puts his fist in the air. "Whoa, Dylan! Studmeister! Give us lessons!"

Chloe laughs and I twirl her around, taking a quick glance at Angie to make sure she's watching. She is.

"Hey, Dylan," Randy says, looking oddly proud of me, "you sure you haven't been smoking Headbone's Hawaiian?"

"No, man," I say, grinning wide. "Unlike you clowns, I'm high on *life*."

Moser and Headbone groan loudly, like this is the lamest thing they've ever heard, but I ignore them, lead Chloe over to Randy, and offer him her hand. She nods approvingly, and he takes it. Mission accomplished.

"Come on, Angie," I say, flashing Nick a sorry-dude-but-you-lose look. I pick up her black canvas camera bag and hike it over my shoulder. "Remember? We've got a movie to shoot."

Five

"SO, ARE YOU IN LOVE WITH HER?" Angie says as we swipe our subway cards and push through the turnstiles at the Ninety-fifth Street station.

"Who, Chloe?"

She rolls her eyes. "Yes, Dylan, who else would I mean?"

I look up for a moment, like I'm mulling this over, then shake my head. "Nah."

"Well, you could have fooled me."

The train is rumbling underground, and as we race down the stairs I'm feeling pretty good about this little turn of events. Now that Chloe's in the picture and Jonathan is out, the shoe is on the other foot. The R wheezes into the station, and I hold the door for Angie. "She's pretty, though," I say. "And talented. *Very* talented."

"Who? Chloe?" Angie asks, brushing past me.

"Ha, ha, very funny."

We transfer to the D at Thirty-sixth Street, and as the train takes off I glance around at the clientele. At first all the passengers seem fairly normal, but soon, at Pacific Street, a guy bearing a strange resemblance to the Tasmanian Devil enters, makes a beeline for the door opposite us, and begins shadowboxing with an imaginary opponent. "Don't look!" I whisper, but of course Angie is already elbowing me while trying to stifle a laugh. "Cut it out!" I say. "You know what happens when nutcases are on the train with me!"

It's a running joke between me and Angie that if a deranged person climbs aboard a New York City subway car that yours truly happens to be riding, like a magnet he will find his way to me. "I can't help it," Angie says. "Look what he's doing now."

I take a quick glance and see that the guy is in the middle of a multipunch combination—left jab into a right uppercut, followed by a left hook. He's no Sly Stallone, but he does know a few things about boxing. Which, considering my track record with lunatics, is not a comforting thought.

Just as Taz and I are about to lock eyes, I quickly purse my lips into a whistle and stare at the string of weight-loss advertisements along the wall. Hopefully, he won't notice my scrawny chest and how little in need I am of a diet. For the next few minutes I manage to maintain a low profile, but as the train slows nearing Grand Street, I glance at Angie and see that she's whipped out her camera and is now digitally recording Taz versus the phantom boxer.

"Angie! Are you out of your mind? Put that thing away!" I whisper.

"No! I'm getting excellent footage."

"Can't you even wait till we get to the park?"

She flashes me a wicked smile. "You know what they say, Dylan. Carpe diem."

I look around for a police officer, but of course there's none available, since they're probably all busting fifteen-year-old guys for things like underwear theft. Taz goes on like this for a while, but as the train comes to a halt he suffers a fatal blow to the jaw, stumbles backward, and falls to the floor. While the carload of passengers looks on, the doors open and an elderly Asian lady carrying two grocery bags stuffed with cabbages, leeks, and bamboo shoots steps over him, shakes her head, and mumbles, "Lousy bum."

"This is awesome!" Angie says, still shooting. "And just think, it's only our first shoot!"

The lady takes a seat across from us, sets down her vegetables, and gives Angie an icy glare. In my opinion, she looks more dangerous than Taz. "Turn. Off. The. Camera," I say to Angie. "Now."

Reluctantly, Angie obeys, setting the camera on her lap, and for the next few minutes Taz continues to lie there motionless. "Dylan," Angie says, nudging me. "I'm getting a little worried. The guy's not moving. He might need CPR. You're still certified, right?"

My father may be a doctor, but that doesn't mean I've inherited his affinity for emergencies, especially those involving blood and body fluids. Just the thought of this guy's saliva in my mouth makes me break out into a cold sweat. "Angie, come on, the guy's not hurt, he's *crazy*!"

Thankfully, as we near West Fourth, Taz wakes from his

stupor. Angie wastes no time; she flips on the camera and begins to record. I glance at the lady with the vegetables, who is eyeing the guy warily. "Must you, really?" I say to Angie.

She nods. "I must."

Right away Taz notices the empty space next to me, hobbles over, and takes a seat. "Man, that was rough," he says. "I swear, that punch came out of nowhere."

Having had plenty of experience with mental cases on the subway, I know that it's best to not completely ignore the guy, but to humor him mildly. I nod. "Mmm, yeah, dude, pretty rough."

"How long was I out?"

I shrug. "Oh, maybe five minutes."

Angie is still shooting, and Taz doesn't seem to mind. In fact, he combs his fingers through his hair and smiles into the camera. "Hey, is this gonna be on TV?"

"Um, well, no," Angie says, "but if you like, it can be included in the short film I'm making." I can't believe she's encouraging this freak.

"Short film, huh? Cool. So what is this now, like an interview?"

The lady with the grocery bags is shaking her head at us. I smile at her apologetically.

Angie nods. "Yes, an interview."

"Okay." Taz fixes his collar. "What do you want to know?"

"Well, let's see," Angie says. "Um, how did you get started in your career?"

Career? She's got to be kidding. The guy is practically

sitting in my lap now, and his breath smells like Tripod's litter box. "Oh, that's easy," he says, taking a few quick jabs. "I grew up on the streets. Been using my fists since I was five years old. When I dropped out of school, Don Turner took me into his gym—Gleason's, up in the Bronx. Been training with him ever since."

I'm not a boxing aficionado, but my buddy Jake and I have watched several fights on HBO, and I happen to know that Don Turner is coach to Evander Holyfield—aka the Real Deal—former Olympian and four-time heavyweight world champ. And yes, he trains at Gleason's Gym. Taz is more deluded than I thought.

"And who was that guy?" Angie goes on. "The one you were just fighting?"

"Oh, him?" Taz jabs his thumb toward the car door like the phantom boxer exited at Grand Street. "Mike Tyson." He shakes his head and laughs a little. "Man, he really put the hurt on me today."

To my relief the train slows down and West Fourth comes into view. I grab Angie's hand and pull her to her feet. "Yeah, well, we've got to go now. See you around, dude."

With Angie in tow, I race along the platform, praying to God that Taz does not follow us. When we reach the stairwell I glance back and see him hanging out the car door. "Hey, the name's Holyfield! Evander Holyfield!"

Angie and I zigzag through the streets of Greenwich Village, which is annoyingly the only section of Manhattan that doesn't follow a grid pattern, and by some miracle wind up at the white stone arch on Fifth Avenue—the triumphal entrance to Washington Square Park. Inside, we pass the hangman's elm (a tree they once used for public executions) and the dog run, where a German shepherd and a golden retriever are playing fetch with a Frisbee, and for a few minutes we watch a very intense chess match at the built-in stone tables at the southwest corner—the place where they filmed that movie *Searching for Bobby Fischer*.

Next we head to the central fountain—a working stage for street performers—and see that a group of mimes dressed like the New York Yankees are about to begin a game of mock baseball against a team of clowns. The whole thing looks pretty cool, so we take seats on the surrounding steps. Angie shoots and I watch.

One by one, the Yankees come up to bat while the clowns make goofy slapstick plays in the outfield. When the bases are finally loaded, number thirteen, "Alex Rodriguez," who surprisingly looks a lot like the real A-Rod, gets up and hits a home run. This appears to be the grand finale, because as the audience cheers, the mimes whip off their baseball caps for tips. Which goes to show you that nothing is actually free in the Big Apple.

Pretty soon A-Rod is making his way toward me. He holds out his baseball cap, and while I dig in my pocket for change, Angie zooms in for a close-up. "So," she says, "what's it like being a street performer in New York City?"

He shrugs and makes a so-so gesture with his free hand.

"He can't talk, Angie," I say. "He's a mime."

"Oh, yeah."

I pull out a few singles and toss one into A-Rod's cap, but apparently this isn't good enough. He stares me down until I fork over the rest. I figure this has to be illegal—extorting tips from minors—but just like the transit cops who are supposed to be hunting down guys like Taz, the officers who should be patrolling the park are probably sipping lattes at the Starbucks across the street.

As A-Rod walks off with every cent I had to my name, Angie slips the camera into her bag and says, "Hey, Dylan, are you hungry?"

Just the mention of food and my stomach begins to growl. I glance at my watch. It's six o'clock, dinnertime. "Yeah, but . . ." I pat my pockets. "I've got nothing left. A-Rod cleaned me out."

"No problem," she says. "My treat. Wait here, I'll be right back." Angie plops the camera bag onto my lap, and before I have a chance to tell her about my recent aversion to things like trans fat, additives, and preservatives, she's running toward a traveling food cart labeled ATHENS EXPRESS parked just outside the arch. The guy manning the cart looks greasier than Moser, and when he opens the grill a cloud of black smoke billows above his head.

Angie returns and hands me a crescent-shaped lump wrapped in aluminum foil. Slowly I peel it open and see that it's a gyro sandwich. Charred flecks decorate the strips of lamb, and suspicious-looking grease is dripping from the bottom. I peer through the haze of smoke in the distance, wondering if Athens Express has ever passed a New York City Board of Health inspection. Not likely. "Um, Angie?" I say. "Do you think this meat is, like, sanitary?"

Angie has already taken a monster-sized bite of her sandwich and is chewing gleefully. Grease runs down her chin. "I have no idea, Dylan. Just eat the gyro. It tastes good."

I peel off a little more foil, wishing there was a label to read. I mean, really, what's *in* this thing? "So what's your moviemaking strategy now?" I say, pointing to a homeless dude with flea-infested dreadlocks and a coat of colorful rags who is standing atop a trash can and welcoming folks into the park. "Interview the Rasta man? Ask him how he got started in his human relations career?"

She licks her fingers and shrugs. "Yeah, maybe."

I sniff the meat and take a rabbit-sized nibble. "Or, better yet"—I motion toward a group of multipierced, multitattooed bikers challenging the regular chess players to a high-stakes match—"how about we film their game until one decides to go postal?"

I expect Angie to laugh, but she doesn't. Instead, she says, "Dylan, what are you so afraid of?"

The question throws me off guard. I take a bigger bite of the gyro and chew. "Nothing. I'm not afraid, Angie. I was making a joke, all right?"

She studies me for a moment, then shakes her head like I'm some kind of lost cause. "All right, fine, whatever."

"What's that supposed to mean?"

She sighs. "Look, Dylan, all I'm saying is that you need to loosen up, take some chances, *live* a little. I mean, when was the last time you did anything remotely spontaneous?"

I take a caveman bite of the gyro and chew hard. "Um, just this afternoon, in case you forgot."

"This afternoon?"

Apparently Angie has a selective memory. "Yes. When I kissed Chloe."

"Ooooh, *that*. Well, I'll admit the kiss was . . . different, definitely out of character for you, but think about it, Dylan, what did you do afterward? Handed her over to Randy like she was his property or something."

I shrug. "So? Randy likes her. And actually, so does Nick, which is why I'm trying to keep Chloe and Nick apart."

Angie looks at me like I'm crazy. "You see, Dylan, that's what I mean. You kissed Chloe because you're *afraid* she's going to hook up with Nick."

I swallow, wishing I had some water to wash down this filthy sandwich. "That's ridiculous, Angie. There's absolutely no logic to what you just said."

I guess Angie reads my mind, because she reaches into her bag and pulls out a bottle of Evian. I take a long swig.

"All right, fine," she says. "Then let me ask you something else. Why are you always trying to protect Randy? Lately all he's been is a screwup. Even before your mother left."

Now, it's fine for me to talk crap about my brother, but when someone else—even a good friend like Angie—calls him a screwup, it's not cool. "You have no idea what you're talking about, Angie. Just give it a rest, okay?"

She shrugs. "Fine, Dylan, suit yourself. But you know what I think? Maybe instead of trying to save Randy, you should figure out who *you* are."

I glare at her and stuff the rest of the gyro into my mouth. As I chug down more water, I see that the Yankees have finished extorting money from the crowd, and now a half-naked Australian guy with spiky blond hair and a huge sun tattoo on his chest is standing atop one of the fountainheads juggling apples. "G'day, mates!" he calls out. "For my opening act I will need one volunteer. Any whackers? Oh, I mean takers! Ha, ha, ha!"

Without even thinking, I wipe the grease from my face, stand up, and raise my hand.

"Aces!" The guy hops off the fountainhead, still juggling the apples. "Come on down, mate! Join me for a little fun."

"Dylan!" Angie says. "What are you doing?"

I turn around. "You know what they say, Angie. Carpe diem."

As I walk toward center stage, the guy starts playing to the crowd. "Down Under we have an expression," he says, " 'She'll be apples.' It means 'Don't worry, love, everything will be all right.' " He waves me on and motions toward the ground. "So lie down, mate, rest your weary bones and . . ." He stops juggling and gives the audience a devilish grin. "She'll be apples!"

Against my better judgment, I stretch out on the warm, pebbly concrete with a strange feeling that my life, as I know it, will never be the same. While the crowd thickens, the Aussie sprints to the sidelines, reaches into an army duffel bag, and pulls out a knife. The blade is a good nine inches long. I lie there frozen while he slices off part of an apple and pops it into his mouth. Chewing vigorously, he pulls out two identical knives and sprints back to me. Straddling my waist, he begins to juggle. "No worries, mate!" He looks up and winks conspiratorially at the crowd. "Remember, she'll be apples! Ha, ha, ha!"

Just when I'm beginning to think this guy might be on crack, I see Angie kneeling beside me. However, she's not here to bail me out. No, my long-lost best friend has turned on her camera and is about to record my execution. Death by decapitation.

I glance at the knives swirling above my head, hard steel glinting in the sun. "So, are you getting some good footage?" I ask.

Angie nods. "Oh, yeah, excellent."

"That's great. Really, I'm happy for you." The blood-thirsty audience is cheering, and suddenly I feel this strange kinship to Russell Crowe in *Gladiator*.

"You doing okay there, mate?" the guy asks.

I don't want him to lose concentration, so I nod and say, "Uh, yeah, I'm fine."

"Okay then, let's see what else we've got in the bag!" He catches all three knives in one hand, then runs to the side-lines to retrieve his next implements of torture.

"Um, Dylan," Angie says, "what do you think he's doing now?"

I watch as the guy pulls out three wooden clubs from his duffel bag. On the end of each club is a large wick. He strikes a match. "Um, he's lighting torches," I say.

"Oh." Angie takes a few steps back and continues shooting. Meanwhile, the Aussie returns looking like an Olympic runner. He straddles me again and begins to juggle. Flames billow over my head. The crowd is really going wild now, and from the corner of my eye I see Angie's Pumas. "Dylan, this is awesome!" she yells.

"Still doing all right there, mate?" the guy asks. He seems completely calm, like we're just shooting the breeze, sharing tea and crumpets or whatever it is those Aussies do.

"Yeah, dude, I'm great, just great."

After juggling the torches, he grabs a set of Lizzie Borden–style hatchets, and as they swing menacingly above my head I hear someone in the crowd call out, "What are you, crazy, man?" The funny thing is I don't know if he's talking to me or to the Aussie. Of course, I realize I can get up and leave at any time, but for some strange reason that's the last thing I want to do.

For the grand finale, the Aussie reaches into his bag and, one by one, pulls out three chain saws. By now, the crowd has tripled in size and the cheers are deafening. "Dylan, get up!" Angie says. "This guy's nuts! He's gone too far!"

I turn and look her square in the eye. "Sorry, Angie, I'm not leaving. Not now."

Before turning on the saws, the Aussie juggles them over my head, testing his dexterity. Next he sets them on the ground beside me and flips on their switches. I look into his face, hoping to see that tea-and-crumpets calmness, but it's not there.

He raises his hands and calls out to the crowd, "Has anyone seen that movie *Texas Chain Saw Massacre*?"

The audience is yelling, but I can't make out what

they're saying because all I hear is the buzzing of the saws. I turn to make sure Angie is shooting. She is.

"Well, guess what?" he says. "*I've* bloody well seen it *three* times! Ha, ha, ha!"

As he picks up the first live chain saw and tosses it over my head, I close my eyes and concentrate on the colors swirling beneath my lids. I'm not sure how much time goes by, but the next thing I know, the Aussie is pulling me to my feet. "Mate," he says, "I forgot to ask, what's your name?"

The sun blinds me. I blink a few times and see that the saws are lying motionless on the ground. I touch my chest and realize that my body is in one piece. "Um, Dylan," I say. "Dylan Fontaine."

He turns to the crowd. "All right, you bloody blokes! Let's hear it for Dylan! Mr. Dylan Fontaine!"

The audience cheers, and for a moment I feel like a celebrity. But soon the Aussie is handing me his empty duffel bag. "Okay, mate, now you're going to collect the cash. Do a good job and we'll split the loot fifty-fifty. Or, uh, something like that." He pushes me toward the crowd and says, "Now, I expect some compensation for this fine act of bravery! So dig deep, pull out those tens, those twenties! Lord knows it's not cheap living in this city!"

I guess it's been a pretty fine show, because as I make my way up the steps, people are patting me on the back and stuffing lots of bills into the bag. Even A-Rod, who stuck around for the act, throws in the singles he extorted from me earlier, plus a few more. I look for Angie and see her waving to me from the sidelines. She's still shooting.

When I'm finished collecting money I give the duffel bag to the Aussie. He smiles, reaches in, and hands me two tens. Of course this is nowhere near half the loot, but it doesn't matter. As I've mentioned before, I, Dylan Fontaine, am not a materialist.

"See that, mate," the Aussie says, plucking an apple from his pile of weapons. He tosses it to me. "Just like I said. She'll be apples."

Six

WITH THE PROCEEDS from my near-death experience, I take Angie to Orgasmic Organics on the corner of Bleecker and MacDougal and order two banana–passion fruit smoothies. I'm not deluded enough to think this drink will stir up actual *passion* in Angie for me, but I do know a few things about the extra shots they can add for fifty cents a pop. So while Angie makes a quick trip to the ladies' room, I ask the guy behind the counter to add a shot of ginseng (natural aphrodisiac of the Orient) to each cup along with a scoop of free-radical-fighting spirulina to combat the effects of the gyro.

When Angie returns I hand her a smoothie, raise my cup in a toast, and say, "Here's to the new Dylan Fontaine— most spontaneous dude on the planet."

Angie nods. "You *rocked* today, Dylan." We each take a long drink. The ginseng is tasteless, but the spirulina is kind of earthy. Angie makes a face. "Dylan, what's in this thing? Cow manure?"

"Well . . ." Since a cow's main staple *is* grass, and spirulina is rather grass*like*, I say, "Yeah, something like that. It's supposed to fight free radicals."

She hands me back the smoothie. "Here, you drink it. I'd much rather die young."

It's getting dark by the time we hop on board the D, and as we cross the Manhattan Bridge toward Brooklyn, I peer out the window and watch the lights sparkle along the water. Strangely, there's something peaceful about being on a crowded subway car, gazing at the Manhattan skyline, especially when Angie is pressed up against me and I can smell faint traces of her green-apple shampoo.

She sighs and leans her head against my shoulder. The double whammy of ginseng is really kicking in now. "Oh, I forgot to tell you, Dylan," she says. "I'm leaving for New Jersey tomorrow. Gotta spend the last week of summer vacation with the G-rents."

It figures that just when Angie gets back, she has to take off to her grandparents' million-dollar mansion in boring old New Jersey. There's a cute little frown on Angie's face, and I have a sudden urge to kiss her. I manage to restrain myself. "That sucks," I say. "When will you be back?"

"Labor Day. After the big backyard barbecue shebang with all the relatives."

"Oh, well, it's going to be rough, but I suppose I can survive one more week without you."

"Yeah, but I might not make it. God, I hate the suburbs."

We transfer to the R. Angie's tired, so I put my arm around her. She closes her eyes and drifts off to sleep. I'm wiped out too, but I stay awake, holding her close, imagining what it would be like if she was actually my girlfriend. When we pull into the Ninety-fifth Street station, I pat her knee and say, "Come on, Sleeping Beauty, it's our stop. I'll walk you home."

We head toward Shore Road and take the scenic route to Angie's house, strolling along the path beside the New York Bay. Angie looks beautiful in the moonlight with the Verrazano Bridge as a backdrop. I begin to wonder if I should tell her how I really feel about her, but as usual I chicken out.

When we reach her house I say, "So I guess we'll take another trip into the Village when you get back from the burbs, huh?"

"Of course." She grins. "Seeing that you're the star of my short film and all."

"Oh? So now I'm your leading man?"

She nods. "You always have been, Dylan." Standing on tiptoe, she plants a kiss on my cheek. "Like I said, you're my best friend. I don't ever want that to change." She reaches up and tousles my hair. "I'll call you when I get back."

One advantage of my father's camping out at the hospital and my mother's taking off with Philippe LeBlanc is that I can come and go as I please. So instead of heading home, I walk along the water, sorting out the events of the day, and after an hour or so I reach the same conclusion I always do: I will never understand girls.

I'm exhausted now and ready for bed, but when I arrive at my house I see two police cars parked directly out front, and my father's Volvo sitting in the driveway at a lopsided angle. At first I think it's Officer Greenwood come to take his revenge, but when I step inside and see the members of the Dead Musicians Society lined up on the sofa and two unknown cops talking to my father in the foyer, I realize it's not me the law is after.

"Dylan!" my dad says. "It's after eleven, where have you been?"

The cops turn around. One is a woman, and even though I shouldn't be having erotic thoughts at a moment like this, I can't help it. She's *hot*. "Um . . ." I look at my dad. What I'm thinking is *When was the last time you even bothered to notice what time I came home?* But I'm not about to give these officers a reason to call in the Bureau of Child Welfare. "I've been in the city, with Angie," I say. "She's shooting a film and wanted me to come along."

My dad's eyes widen. "A film? With Angie? Well, that explains it, then." He turns to the cops. "Angie is Dylan's friend who spent the summer at NYU. She's a very responsible girl." I guess my dad is trying to prove that he has at least one son who is not a juvenile delinquent, but the cops don't seem very impressed. He clears his throat. "Dylan, this is Officer Mertz and Officer Olson." The three of us nod hellos. "They may want to ask you a few questions. Why don't you have a seat with the others for now?" He motions toward

Randy and his friends. I'm wondering what all this is about, but considering the fact that my brother and his band engage in illegal activities on a daily basis, I figure it can't be good.

"Um . . . okay, Dad." There's no room left on the sofa, so I take a seat on the armrest next to Headbone. Chloe, I notice, is sitting cross-legged on the floor at the far end playing with stray carpet threads. I give Randy a what's-up look. He nods as if to say *Chill, bro, it's all gonna go down easy, you'll see.*

While my dad and the police officers continue their hushed conversation in the foyer, I take a closer look at Officer Olson—a stunning brunette with exotic eyes who looks incredibly sexy with that gun and holster strapped around her hips. Mertz—your typical middle-aged New York City cop, complete with beer gut and cynical smile—has scored big having her as his partner. Lucky guy.

While I'm in the middle of a fantasy that involves unbuckling the aforementioned holster, Headbone elbows me. "Dylan, we're all counting on you to smooth this police chick. Just turn on your studmeister magic and she'll be putty in your hands."

Suddenly Chloe's head pops out from behind the sofa. "Hey, I heard that, Headbone!"

"Oops, sorry, Clo," he says. "It's just, well, the Vagina Head doesn't seem to be doing too well at the moment." He peers toward the foyer. "Hey, you don't think Olson's one of those lesbian cops, do you? I mean, not all of them are butch, you know."

"God! Why do I tolerate you morons?" Chloe stands,

gives us all a disgusted glare like she is fed up with the entire male population, and storms into the kitchen.

Moser, whose eczema really flares up under stress, is scratching away. On the coffee table is a tube of prescription cortisone cream that my dad must have given him, but it doesn't seem to be doing the job. The left side of his face is swollen, and it looks like he may need a shot of Benadryl, maybe even epinephrine. "I knew I shouldn't have let you guys drag me into that shower! Look at me!"

Nick is sitting at the far end next to Moser, and for a guy who's usually cool and unflappable, he's looking rather peaked. Beads of sweat cover his forehead and upper lip. This worries me.

I lean over to Randy and whisper, "What's going on?"

He sighs. "Nothing much. That old lady across the street, Mrs. Underwood, called the cops on us. Said her poodle was freaking out from all the noise over here."

I glare at Headbone, who always smashes his drums and cymbals way too loud. He shrugs. "Sorry, dude, I was in a zone, what can I say?"

But still, this doesn't explain why Nick is sweating bullets. "And that's it?" I say. "They're here because of some noise?"

"Well, not exactly," Randy says. "Mrs. Underwood also told the cops that she smelled"—he pauses and rolls his eyes—"*mar-i-juana* coming from our house this morning when she was walking her yappy runt."

Headbone shakes his head. "I swear, people need to mind their own business in this neighborhood."

"Oh, that's just great," I say. "Anything *else* I should know?"

Randy looks away while Moser picks up the cortisone tube and squeezes a gob onto his finger. "Um, Randy?" Moser says. "You might want to tell Dylan about the golf cart situation. You know, just in case the cops ask."

"Golf cart?" I say. I know Randy and his friends sometimes sneak out in the middle of the night and get high on the golf course, but I didn't think they were stupid enough to take any joyrides.

Randy frowns. "Yeah, well, it seems there's a golf cart missing from the Shore Road Golf Club. They're asking if we know anything about it."

"And . . . do you?"

No one says anything, but soon Headbone is grinning. "Dyl, no sweat, man, we just had a little fun last night. We were gonna give it back."

Now Mertz, Olson, and my dad walk over to us, and even though my dad looks at women's bodies in his office all day long, even *he* can't keep his eyes off Olson's holster swaying from side to side. Apparently Olson is a take-charge kind of lady, because without consulting Mertz she whips out a pen and pad of paper from her back pocket and says, "Okay, Dylan, I've already spoken with your brother and his friends. Now I'd like to ask you some questions."

Headbone elbows me again and whispers, "All right, Dyl, kick it into high gear."

Olson slides the pen cap off with her teeth. Her lips are covered in shiny pink gloss, and I try not to think about how kissable they are. "Your father tells me that your mother is in Paris with a friend. They have an art show together? Is this correct?"

I look at my dad, but he's staring at the floor. "Um, yes, that's correct," I say, "but I don't see what that has to do with—"

She holds up one hand. "I'm just trying to establish a few facts here, Dylan. Both you and your brother are juveniles, so I need to get an idea of your living situation." She scribbles something down. "Now, moving right along, we've had some complaints from a neighbor, not only about the noise, but about the smell of marijuana coming from this house. Also, there's a golf cart missing from the Shore Road Golf Club. Do you know anything about these incidents?"

"Um . . ." I furrow my brow, like I'm deep in thought, wondering if a cop like Olson can give a kid like me a lie-detector test against my will. "No," I say, "I don't know anything."

She nods and takes a few more notes. "All right, then. Officer Mertz and I are going to have a few words in private with your father; after that we should be finished."

While the three of them disappear into my father's den, I glance at Nick, who looks like he's on the wrong end of a firing squad. "What's the matter, Nick?" I say. "I mean, this isn't your house. It's not like your ass is on the line."

He narrows his eyes at me. "What's the *matter*, Dylan, is that your brother, who happens to be my best friend, could be in a lot of trouble right now. And I'm not about to let him take the rap for all of us."

I suppose in his own sinister way, Nick really does care about Randy, but I'm not buying any of his philanthropic bullcrap. "Fine," I say, "whatever. I'm gonna get something to eat. Call me when they come out, all right?"

Headbone gives me his signature slap-grip handshake. "Sure thing, Dyl. And listen, you did all right by Olson. She's one tough chick."

In the kitchen, Chloe is sitting at the table, flipping through one of my dad's medical journals. I notice that the article she's reading is about birth control pills. She glances up from the page and says, "Dylan, take a look in the garage."

First I peer into the hallway to make sure the cops are still in the den; then, very slowly, I crack open the door to the garage. Lo and behold, there is a golf cart labeled SHORE ROAD GOLF CLUB parked next to my mom's Honda—the one she left behind, since Philippe LeBlanc's landlord only allows one car per apartment. "Oh, God," I say, closing the door and turning the lock.

"Yeah," Chloe says, "my thoughts exactly."

I've lost my appetite now, so I join Chloe at the table and play with the salt and pepper shakers. Soon I hear the door of the den swing open. Chloe remains seated, but I go out into the hallway. My dad stands beside a potted plant in the adjoining dining room, nervously running his fingers through his hair, while Mertz hunkers down next to Randy, and Olson scribbles in her pad nearby. "Randy," Mertz says, "your father has agreed to let us search your room. He feels that if you have been using drugs, there should be consequences."

At first, I think I don't hear right. I mean, my dad knows that Randy stashes weed in his room. Why would he want the police to find it? Randy blinks a few times and turns to my dad, but my dad won't look at him.

"Wait a minute!" Headbone says, glancing back and forth between Mertz and Olson. "You guys can't do that! I know the law! You can't go into his room without a search warrant! Dr. Fontaine, these police officers are clearly taking advantage of you!" Before Headbone started doing drugs last year, he was ranked number three at his old school. In dire situations, he still sounds like a person with active brain cells.

Olson looks up from her pad. "Yes, Arthur," she says, "that's true in most cases, but this is Dr. Fontaine's house and he has agreed to a search. In fact, he is highly in favor of it. Isn't that correct, Dr. Fontaine?"

My dad nods; his face is flushed and his hair is sticking up at odd angles. "Yes, that's correct," he says.

"And we should probably inform you, Randy," Olson continues, "that Officer Mertz and I are both highly trained in this field. If there are drugs in your room, they *will* be found."

A comforting thought. Randy is staring at the ground now, and I can't tell whether he's scared or just plain pissed. He and my dad have been on pretty bad terms lately, but I never thought my dad would turn traitor.

I glance toward the kitchen, wondering if Mertz and Olson are also highly trained in finding stolen golf carts, and that's when I see Chloe tiptoeing to the stairs.

I assume she's planning to remove the incriminating evidence from Randy's room, so I have to act fast. "Um, wait a second!" I say. All eyes turn in my direction. "Before you do anything, I need to talk to my father. In private."

Reluctantly, Mertz and Olson nod in agreement while I cross the room. "What's this about, Dylan?" my dad whispers. "The police officers don't have all night."

"I don't care about *them*," I say. "I care about *Randy*. Why are you doing this to him?"

"Dylan," my dad says sternly, "Randy's gotten himself into this mess, and I'm not going to bail him out. What I'm doing here is called tough love. And right now he needs a huge dose of it."

I stare at him long and hard. "Tough love? So what happened to loyalty? A family sticking together? Blood being thicker than water?" Considering the fact that my mother has abandoned us, I feel the sting of my own words. And now I'm not even thinking about what Chloe is doing upstairs. I want answers.

"Yes, Dylan, I believe in those things too, but right now Randy needs something entirely different. I've already spoken to the officers. We're not talking jail time here, just probation, counseling, and monthly drug testing. Believe me, it's for the best."

"Yeah, except that he'll hate you for the rest of his life."

My dad sighs. "It's true that Randy may hate me for a while, but I don't think it will be for the rest of his life."

I'm not so sure about that. I consider arguing the point further, but from the look on my dad's face I realize there's nothing I can do.

"Dr. Fontaine?" Olson says. "Should we begin?"

My dad motions toward the stairs. "Yes, please do."

"Wait! Hold on!" I blurt out. Stalling for time, I add,

"Why search only Randy's room? Why not mine, too? I mean, that's only fair, right?"

"Dylan," my dad says sternly. "I don't think that will be necessary."

"Come on, Dad, think about it. *I* was the one arrested yesterday. The cops found weed in *my* pocket." Obviously, this is news to Olson and Mertz, who, up until now, were probably feeling sorry for me for having been born into such a dysfunctional family. While both of them hike their eyebrows, I glance at the stairs. *Hurry, Chloe, please, hurry.* I hope she knows Randy's hiding places—under the plastic mat of his old Twister game, at the bottom of a skuzzy bottle labeled IRON FILINGS, inside his old chemistry set next to a box of condoms—ribbed, lubricated, and, sadly for him, unopened.

"Dr. Fontaine?" Olson says. "Is this true? Was Dylan arrested yesterday?"

My dad shakes his head. "No, no, you don't understand. I mean, he was, but that was all just . . . a mix-up, really. Dylan does *not* use drugs."

Mertz cocks his head. "How do you know that for sure?"

"Well, because I trust him and . . . oh, of course, you can check it out yourself. Call the precinct. Ask to speak with Lieutenant Burns. Dylan's urine test was clear. They didn't press charges."

From the corner of my eye I catch a glimpse of Chloe tiptoeing back into the kitchen. I breathe a huge sigh of relief. "But Dad," I say. "I still think they should search my room. It's the right thing to do."

Randy and Nick are looking at me like I'm insane, but Moser and Headbone seem to think I'm a hero. "Dylan, my man!" Headbone says. "You are, like, the *bomb*! Way to stick up for your brother!"

Moser nods. "That's loyalty, *compadre*."

"Um, Dr. Fontaine," Mertz says, "considering the information Dylan just shared, maybe it would be a good idea if we searched both boys' rooms."

My father sighs deeply. "Fine, whatever, I really don't care at this point. Search the whole damn house if you want."

I panic, thinking about the golf cart, but thankfully Olson says, "That won't be necessary, Dr. Fontaine. The boys' rooms will be enough."

While the two of them head upstairs, my dad exhales loudly and plunks onto a dining room chair. I take my seat on the armrest next to Headbone, and the six of us wait in silence. In the kitchen I hear Chloe flipping the pages of the medical journal.

"Dr. Fontaine?" Mertz says, after what seems like an eternity. He and Olson pad down the steps. My dad stands up; he looks awful—like he hasn't slept in days, which may very well be the case. "We didn't find anything. In either of the boys' rooms."

My dad nods and says nothing. Nick sits back, relieved, and Moser and Headbone give each other low fives. Randy sits there, expressionless.

Chloe is smiling in the kitchen doorway. Our eyes meet for a brief second, and I smile back.

Meanwhile, Olson walks over and hands my dad a slip of pink paper. "It's been an interesting evening, Dr. Fontaine," she says. "This is a warning notice about the noise level." She looks at the five of us lined up on the sofa. "Gentlemen, I hope I won't be hearing any further complaints from the neighbors?"

"Oh, you got it," Headbone says, giving her a thumbs-up. "Definitely, no more complaints."

She nods. "Well, if that's the case, this should be the last time we meet."

As my dad ushers Mertz and Olson to the foyer, I watch Olson's hips sashay out the door. "Hey, I wouldn't mind meeting up with her again," Headbone says, "under different circumstances, of course."

When my dad returns, he stands there for a long time giving Randy and his friends the evil eye. I know what he's thinking—if Randy didn't hang out with these morons, our lives might be normal. There was a time when he used to kick them out of our house on a regular basis. But they always came back. After a while I guess he realized he couldn't choose Randy's friends. Now they're like a fixture in our home, an eyesore that you get used to. My dad sighs deeply. "Randy, Dylan. I'm going to bed. We will discuss this situation tomorrow. The rest of you, *leave. Now.* And I don't want to see your faces for a long time. Understood?"

Nick is the first to stand up. "Yes, Dr. Fontaine, we understand. And we're sorry about everything."

Headbone chimes in. "Yeah, *really* sorry. It won't happen again."

Moser holds up the tube of cortisone. "I apologize too, Dr. Fontaine. And thank you for the medicine. It's helping, um, sort of."

My dad walks over to Moser with a look of concern and examines the red patches on his face. Not only are his doctorly instincts kicking in, but I think deep down he's got a soft spot for Moser and Headbone. "Just keep using the cream every two to three hours, Moser. Oh, and one more thing." He pulls out a pad of paper from his pocket, scribbles something down, and rips out a sheet. "Use this next time you shower. It's a prescription for hypoallergenic soap."

Moser looks like he's about to faint. "Did you say . . . shower?"

"Yeah, dude," Headbone says. "We've got a girl in our band now. Showering is, like, mandatory."

From the kitchen doorway Chloe chimes in, "Don't worry, Dr. Fontaine. I'll make sure Moser gets the right soap."

"Thank you, Chloe," my dad says. "And now, all of you, go!"

While my dad trudges to his room, Randy steps outside with his friends, and after a chorus of goodbyes, I hear him and Nick talking in hushed voices on the front patio. I strain my ears to listen, but since I can't make out what they're saying, I give up and head upstairs to bed.

In the hallway I hear Tripod meowing from inside my mom's studio. "Stupid cat!" I say, pushing open the door. "She's not here, you idiot, and she's not coming back. Don't you realize that by now?"

Tripod rushes past me, and I see that he has knocked over some art supplies on my mother's desk. I go inside, and as I set them back in place I notice that the small antique table has been moved. Instead of being next to my mother's computer, it's beside the picture window. For some reason this bothers me, and as I push the table back to its original spot, I trip on a loose floorboard that was directly underneath it.

I kneel down and remove the board, along with two loose planks on either side of it. Hidden under it I find a metric scale engraved with the words PROPERTY OF MCKINLEY HIGH SCIENCE DEPARTMENT. Next to the scale is a gallon-sized Ziploc bag of Hawaiian purple-bud sinsemilla, which, according to Arthur Wellington III, aka Headbone, is the most potent weed on the planet.

And then it hits me. Randy is dealing.

Seven

TALK ABOUT IRONY AND INJUSTICE. While the Dead Musicians Society is racking up felonies without consequence, yours truly, poster boy for a better America, must stand before a judge in court Monday morning, plead guilty to shoplifting, and accept the terms of my punishment—a whopping two-hundred-dollar fine, along with twenty hours of community service.

Upon hearing this, my father drives to the bank that very afternoon and withdraws two hundred dollars from Randy's account—money he's been saving for a new Stratocaster guitar—and pays the fine. I suppose it's his way of making Randy feel the pain of his misdeeds, but it doesn't seem to work. In fact, when Randy finds out, he just shrugs and says, "It figures the Vagina Head's weapon of choice would be the almighty dollar." Since I know how much Randy wants that new Strat, his reaction only furthers my belief that he is making a buttload of cash off the purple bud stashed in my mom's studio.

"I know what you're doing," I say, "and the cops are going to find it, you'll see." It's Tuesday morning, the day after my humiliating experience in court, and Randy and I are sitting at the breakfast table. I'm in a rush, sucking down a soy protein shake like a madman so I can hop the bus to the Staten Island YMCA—my chosen venue for community service—and get there by 10 a.m.

"What are you talking about?" Randy says, chewing a spoonful of cereal. Normally he wouldn't be up this early, but the guys and Chloe are coming over to practice for their big gig this weekend. "I already told you, Dyl. Headbone got rid of the golf cart. He and Moser drove it back to the club last night. They even charged up the battery. No one knows who took it. Everything's cool."

I glare at him. "That's *not* what I'm talking about."

"Then what *are* you talking about?"

"The *weed*, Randy. Upstairs. I'm not an idiot."

He shakes his head and eats another spoonful of cereal. "Listen, Dyl, there's nothing in my room. Chloe took what I had and flushed it. And you don't have to worry about the police because now I've got the perfect hiding spot for my stash in the backyard. And the best part is"—he grins—"it's not even on our property. If the cops dig it up, old man Pellegrino gets busted."

I am tempted to hurl the rest of my shake at him, but I don't. Instead I drink it down, slam the glass on the table, and stand up. "You're *pathetic*, you know that, Randy? Both you *and* your stupid friends! I mean, *why* are you even doing this? Is it because you want to be some major badass? Or is it just for the thrill? To see how much you can get away with?" I shove in my chair, and it almost topples over. "And besides, what do you need the money for? Doesn't Dad give you enough?"

Randy sits there with his mouth hanging open. He sets down his spoon. "Whoa, Dylan. I don't know what you're talking about, but you seriously need to get a *grip*. You're all strung out. I've never seen you like this before."

I grab my wallet and head for the door. "Yeah, well, get used to it, Randy. 'Cause this is the new *me*."

The reason I chose to do community service at the YMCA instead of the dog pound or the homeless shelter or the local church is because I figured I could shoot hoops in the gym during my free time—stay on top of my game for the AAU finals this weekend. But when I show up for work and meet my new boss, Mr. Pickler, my hopes go down the drain; and after two minutes in his office I decide that smelly dogs, winos, even nuns on a mission to save me from the pit of hell would be welcome company compared to this guy.

"Dylan, you *do* realize it's a privilege to be here, correct?" Mr. Pickler says. He's sitting at his desk, tapping a pencil and shuffling through my paperwork.

I'm in a chair across from him, trying to appear penitent. It's not easy. "Um . . . yes, sir, I suppose I do." On the wall behind him is a cheesy piece of art—a Thomas Kinkade print entitled *Mountain Paradise*—which speaks volumes about Pickler's lack of taste and artistic appreciation. I can't help it; I make a face.

"Is there a problem, Mr. Fontaine?"

"No, sir."

He lowers his bifocals and narrows his eyes, letting me know just how much he despises wiseass teenagers. "Well, in that case, I don't have to explain that you are here to *work* and not to goof off. The facilities are for our members and their guests *only*. Understood?"

Just like I thought. There goes hoop practice. "Yes, sir, I understand."

"Very well then, about your responsibilities . . ."

I keep my eye on the clock while he lectures me for an hour or so about the importance of punctuality, respectfulness, and performing my duties within a reasonable time frame. By the end, I wonder if this guy actually does any work himself.

"Um, Mr. Pickler?" I say. We're in the hallway now, and he's rummaging through a closet of cleaning supplies.

"Yes, Dylan? Ah, there it is." He turns around and hands me a scrub brush and a bottle of bleach.

"I was wondering, does the time we spent, you know, *talking* count toward the twenty hours?"

He arches an eyebrow. "*That*, Dylan, will be decided at the end of the day. Right now the bathrooms are waiting. I'll be inspecting your work shortly, and when you're finished, both gyms need to be swept." He pauses for a moment, eyeing the bleach. "I, uh, trust you will not be *sniffing* anything on the job?"

At first I don't realize what he's talking about, and then

it dawns on me: Pickler thinks I might inhale the cleaning supplies to get high. Unbelievable. Even Headbone and Moser are not *that* hard-core. I shake my head. "Oh, no, Mr. Pickler, you've got it all wrong. Besides, I'm not here on drug charges."

"Oh?"

"You mean they didn't tell you why I got arrested?"

He shakes his head. "No, the staff here is never informed as to why someone is doing community service. Unless, of course, they're a sex offender."

"Oh . . . right."

As I'm digesting this piece of information and thinking that I'd better stay away from any strange-looking dudes in the men's locker room, Pickler gives me a meaningful look. "You see, Dylan, since part of my job is to encourage the rehabilitation of our workers, I try to spend quality time with them. In most cases they open up, talk about their problems, and I find that the majority of boys your age are here on substance abuse charges."

He watches me for a while, and I begin to realize that Pickler is very interested in the particulars of my crime. In fact, he's downright nosy. Since the last thing I want is a heart-to-heart with this guy, I decide to give him an excellent reason to stay away. "Well," I say, "it's a little embarrassing, sir, but I'm here because I stole underwear."

His eyes widen.

"A certain *kind,* if you know what I mean." Notice, I didn't lie.

He stands there, blinking. "Well, Dylan, that *is* rather . . . unusual."

"Yes, sir, I know."

He takes a step back. "I, uh, probably wouldn't share that bit of information with any of the staff here. Just . . . keep it to yourself, okay?"

"Oh, sure thing, Mr. Pickler. I *totally* understand." I raise the bottle of bleach and the brush. "Better get to work now. I'll let you know when I'm done."

Pickler leaves me alone for most of the week, but even so, I don't slack off. Each day I show up at 10 a.m.—clean toilets, sweep floors, wash windows, basically do whatever Pickler thinks will reform my deviant soul—and hop back on the bus by 3 p.m. This gets me home before rush hour, and also gives me time to shoot hoops with Jake and the guys later in the evening. So, even though community service sucks, I have to admit that staying busy 24/7 helps keep my mind off Randy and the drug trafficking that seems to be going on in my own house.

By the time Friday morning rolls around, I'm pretty psyched. In exactly five hours I'll be finished paying my debt to society, and if I'm lucky will never have to set eyes on Mr. Pickler again. But as it turns out, my buddy Jake has other plans for me. At noon he walks into the gym. "Hey, it's the criminal! Put down that broom and let's play some ball!"

"Jake?" I say. "What are you doing here?" I glance around; thankfully, Pickler is nowhere in sight.

Jake sprints over and claps me on the back. "Listen to this, Dylan. Our team got some players from Monroe High to meet us here for a scrimmage. The guys are in the locker room right now getting ready." He raises both hands. "Pretty awesome, huh? Today I brought the Titans to *you!*"

"But Jake, I can't play right now, you know that. I have to work until three. And I told you about Pickler. He's *nuts!*"

Jake waves this away like it's nothing. "Aw, come on, Dylan, don't wimp out on me. Tomorrow's our big game. And besides, wait till you hear *this*. Coach Robinson is here. I saw him at the front desk, told him about the scrimmage, and he wants to see our game. Said he's scouting right now for his varsity players for the fall."

"Really?" Last year on JV, it seemed like Coach Robinson was either checking on stats or jawing with a ref when I made my best plays. Now is my chance to show him what I can do.

Suddenly the guys come stampeding onto the court. Mike Pappas hits a reverse layup and calls out, "Hey, Fontaine! Where's your orange jumpsuit? Your ball and chain?" The rest of them start laughing.

I look at Jake. "Thanks for spreading the word, dude. Really, I owe you one."

"Chill out, Dylan. They're just joking around." He hands me a bag. "Here. I stopped by your house and got your jersey and shorts. Hurry up and change."

Coach Robinson is in the bleachers when I come back. As I sprint over to the guys, Jake announces, "Let's hear it for the Titans' starting forward! Number thirty-four, Dylan Fontaine!"

The team cheers and Coach Robinson sits up a little taller. "Whoa, Fontaine!" he calls. "What'd you do, grow a foot this summer?"

"Yeah," I say, trying hard not to grin. "Something like that." Pickler is still nowhere in sight, and I'm pretty sure he wouldn't even recognize me now that I'm in uniform.

After a ten-minute warm-up we start the game. One thing I know about Coach Robinson is that he likes team players, so instead of going for the glory, I make solid passes, get plenty of rebounds, and play a tight defense. We win 41–38, and when Coach comes to the sidelines to congratulate our team, I feel pretty good about how I played. At first, he doesn't single out anyone, but after a while he takes me aside. "I like what I saw on the court today, Fontaine. You're a good, solid player, and Lord knows, you've got the height. Keep working and there may be a spot for you on varsity this fall."

"Thank you, sir. I will. I'll work hard."

A few yards away, Jake is giving me the thumbs-up. Things seem to be going pretty well until Pickler walks into the gym. "Hey, Coach Robinson!" he says. "Nice to see you!"

Great. Pickler knows Coach. In fact, they seem to be chums. Coach gives him a friendly wave, but soon Pickler realizes that it's me standing next to him. "Dylan?" He marches over, eyeing my jersey. "You *know* you are *not* supposed to be using the facilities. You're here to work." He glances at the clock. "You've got two more hours. Actually, three, since you've obviously been goofing off."

Coach is confused. "Um, is there a problem, Mr. Pickler?"

Pickler sighs. "Well, yes, actually. Dylan is here for community service. He's not supposed to be playing ball."

"Community service?" Coach looks at me and grins. "Jeez, what'd you do, Fontaine? Forget to help a little old lady across the street?"

"Um . . . well, not exactly," I say.

While Coach waits for an explanation, Picker begins to smirk. I have a sneaking suspicion that Pickler can't wait to spill the beans about my crime—about the certain *type* of underwear I stole. I could kick myself for being such a wiseass. "Well, Dylan," Pickler says, "I believe the front hallway needs mopping. I suggest you change back into your work clothes and begin."

"Yes, Mr. Pickler," I say. "Bye, Coach. Thanks again."

Glumly I walk to the exit door, and when I turn around I see Pickler whispering to Coach Robinson. Coach looks up, stunned. We lock eyes. I kiss varsity ball goodbye.

Eight

WHEN I ARRIVE HOME—hungry, tired, and convinced that I am the biggest jerk on the planet—I hear the Dead Musicians Society in the basement playing Jimi Hendrix's "Voodoo Child." The kitchen is littered with dirty dishes, empty beer bottles, and a variety of pot paraphernalia, and there is a note from my dad taped to the refrigerator. It reads: *There's a full moon tonight so Labor & Delivery is already a zoo. If I'm lucky I'll see you guys in the morning. Dad.* Inside the fridge is the pan of vegetable lasagna I made last night, but when I peel back the foil, I find out that, except for a spattering of tomato sauce and few stray mushrooms, it's empty.

All of this, combined with Coach Robinson believing that I like to dress in women's underwear, and the fact that the police might show up soon to arrest my brother, is enough to put any guy over the edge. But when I hit the Incoming button on our phone's answering machine, hoping to hear a message from Angie about her sucky time in the burbs and how much she misses me, instead I hear a distantly familiar voice say, *"Hi, guys, it's me, Mom, calling from Paris. The art show is going very well, and as it turns out, Philippe and I may have to stay a bit longer—"* I decide I've had enough. I stop the message midsentence, grab a basketball from the garage, and march downstairs.

The guys are really into the music and for a while they don't even realize I'm there. Moser's head is bobbing up and down as he plays a loud, steady bass line, and Headbone is magically keeping rhythm to a song that seems to move all around the room. Randy holds his guitar, effortlessly sliding his fingers up and down the frets, while Nick, all sweaty, belts out *"Well, I stand up next to a mountain, and I chop it down with the edge of my hand. . . ."* The only one missing is Chloe, which is no surprise, really, considering the state of the kitchen.

I take a seat atop the banister, waiting, gripping my basketball until my knuckles turn white. Apparently my father's recent threat didn't faze Randy's friends at all. Not only are they back, they're high, and as Nick belts out the chorus, *"'Cause I'm a Voodoo Child . . . ,"* it really hits me how unfair life can be. I mean here's a guy who lives on Pop-Tarts, Dr Pepper, and reefer, and just because he's lead singer in a band and occasionally lifts a few dumbbells, he winds up with the build of Brad Pitt in *Fight Club* and has all the babes, including Chloe, falling all over him. But as I continue to listen to the music, I realize that what pisses me off the most is how good they all sound—my brother best of all.

When the song is over, I throw the basketball at Randy. It grazes his right shoulder, bounces off his amp, and smashes into Headbone's cymbals. They all look up. "Dylan!" Randy shouts. "What's going on, man? What's wrong with you?"

"Nothing's wrong with me." I jump off the banister and look him straight in the eye. "And what's going on is this: you and I, right now, are gonna go outside and have a game of one-on-one."

"What?" He laughs. "You want to play basketball? Dylan, come on, man, do you need to talk or something? You've been acting pretty crazy lately."

Headbone picks up the ball. "Yeah, dude, you all right? You're looking kind of strange."

I grab the ball from Headbone. "Yes, Headbone, I'm fine." I turn back to Randy. "And *no*, I do *not* need to talk. In fact, *talking* is the last thing I want to do right now."

They all stare at me like I've completely lost my mind. Then Moser flashes me a guilt-ridden smile, revealing a tell-tale piece of spinach stuck between his two front teeth. "Hey, uh, Dyl," he says, "if this is about the vegetable lasagna, which was really good, by the way, we're sorry. And if you want to know the truth, it was Headbone who finished off the last piece. I told him not to, but—"

"Hey!" Headbone says. "Get it straight, Moser, you ate half the pan!"

Nick sets down his guitar and looks at me like he's all concerned about his best friend's little brother, but he can't fool me. "Dylan," he says, "you *are* looking pretty strung out.

Did something happen at the Y? Something with Pickler? Do you want to talk about it?"

I'm not in the mood for Nick's Freudian psychobabble. "No, *nothing* happened. And if you don't mind, *Nick*, this is between me and my brother, all right? So stay out of it."

"Ooooooo," Headbone says. "This appears serious."

It seems that Randy doesn't like the way I spoke to his best bud and fellow band member. He walks over and swipes the ball from my hand. "All right, Dylan, if that's what you want, fine, we'll play some one-on-one." He waves to his friends. "Come on, guys, let's go."

The five of us head outside to the driveway, where, years ago, my dad sank a basketball pole into the ground for Randy and me. You'd never know it now, but Randy was a starter on his middle school team and even played part of freshman year. That was before he got ultraserious with the Dead Musicians Society and way too cool for team sports. Anyway, back then we played a lot together, and because Randy was always taller and stronger than me, he usually won. Today, however, I have the clear advantage. Not only have I grown half a foot this year, but while Randy was smoking dope all summer, I was lifting weights and playing AAU ball.

Nick, Headbone, and Moser take seats along the driveway while Randy and I face each other under the net. "Twenty-one-point game," I say. "You get possession first."

Randy laughs. "Sorry, Dylan. I know you think you're *all that*, but let me tell you something. Playing basketball is like riding a bike. Two seconds and it all comes back." He throws the ball at me, hard. "It's your possession."

"Hey, do you guys need me to ref?" Headbone calls from the sidelines. " 'Cause I'd say you're both looking pretty psycho right now."

"No ref," I say, keeping my eyes on Randy. "In this game, *anything* goes."

Randy nods. "I'm down with that."

Moser stands up and scratches his armpit. "Hey, you guys are making me nervous. I mean, what happened to the Dead Musicians Society's code of honor? I thought we were all about love and peace and—"

"Shut up, Moser!" Randy says. He turns to me. "Now, let's play ball!"

My adrenaline is pumping, and it feels like every cell in my body is on fire. I take the ball and right away fake Randy out, run past him, and score an easy layup. On the sidelines I see Nick, Moser, and Headbone with their eyes popping out, and when I steal the ball from Randy and score again, I hear them moan. Next Randy tries faking me out, but I call his bluff, put up a solid defense, and block his shot; he falls to the ground. "Hey, that's a foul!" Headbone yells.

"Dylan!" Nick shouts. "It's not cool to play dirty, man! Especially against your own brother!"

I toss the ball to Randy and walk directly up to Nick. "Well, guess what, Nick? Right now I don't need *you* or anyone else telling *me* how to play basketball. So keep your mouth *shut*. Got it?"

Nick glares at me but keeps his cool and, surprisingly, backs off. I walk onto the court with a feeling of invincibility. This doesn't last long, because a few minutes later, Randy wakes from his drug-induced stupor and starts putting the moves on me. He drives in hard and scores, then boxes me out, steals the ball, and makes a reverse hook shot. With each play the game gets rougher, and when Randy takes the lead, I grab the ball and charge him like a raging bull. We both fall to the ground.

"What's your problem, dude?" he screams.

I'm lying on top of Randy; the heels of my hands are all torn up, and Randy's right elbow is bleeding. I grab his wrists and pin him to the ground. "The only one who has a problem, *dude*, is *you!*"

Randy seems to have superhuman strength, because he breaks free, puts two hands on my chest, and gives me a powerful shove. I fall back and hit my head against the pole. Everything starts to spin. Next thing I know, he's standing over me. "So what is it, Dylan? What do you think my problem is? Except for the fact that I might kill you!"

My ears are ringing, but I manage to stand up. I'm a little wobbly. I feel a warm trickle run down the back of my scalp. "Why don't you write songs anymore?" I blurt out.

Randy stands there blinking. "What did you say?"

"You heard me." I point to Nick, Headbone, and Moser. "Why do you waste your time playing music with a bunch of stoners who don't—"

"Hey, I resent that!" Headbone shouts.

"Shut up, Headbone!" I say. I turn back to Randy. "Who

don't have *half* the talent you do? Think about it, Randy, you play *dead* people's music. And why is that? Are *you* dead? 'Cause ever since Mom left, you—"

Suddenly Randy's fist connects with my face and I am back on the ground seeing stars. I scramble to my feet and pounce on him, and then it's pure mayhem. It could be my imagination, but in the midst of the fight I think I hear a girl screaming, "Break it up, you assholes!" I manage to get a few good punches in before Nick, Moser, and Headbone pull me and Randy off each other.

As I sit there tasting blood and feeling a little nauseated, I see Chloe, hands on her hips, shaking her head at the two of us. "Well, well," she says, "what do you know, it's Cain and Abel. Is this what you guys do for fun when I'm not around?"

Headbone throws up his hands. "Clo, I swear to God, we tried to stop them, I even offered to ref the game, but they just wanted to kill each other!"

I'm breathing hard and my chest hurts. "Does Chloe know?" I say to Randy.

Randy's lip is busted, and little pebbles from the driveway are embedded in his right cheek. "Know *what?*"

"That you're dealing."

His eyes widen and he starts to laugh. "Dealing? As in drugs? Is that what you think I'm doing?"

Every member of the Dead Musicians Society, including Chloe, is staring at me with their mouths hanging open. "Dylan," Moser says, "you are seriously mistaken, man. I mean, sure Randy and the rest of us occasionally *smoke* the

stuff, well, maybe more than occasionally, but we're not stupid enough to deal. It's not like we're into capitalism or anything. Our band's not about the legal tender."

"Yeah," Headbone says, "we just do a little mind altering from time to time, all in the name of music, of course."

Nick gives me a strange look. "Dylan, what makes you think Randy's dealing?"

"It's not what I *think*, Nick, it's what I *know*." I look at Randy. "You even admitted it the other day. Remember? You said your stash was buried on Mr. Pellegrino's property."

Randy rolls his eyes. "My own *personal* stash, Dyl. An ounce, maybe, that's all. And I was only joking about old man Pellegrino. Besides, do you really think the cops would bust a ninety-year-old World War Two veteran?"

"All right then, what about the huge bag of purple-bud under the floorboards in Mom's studio, and the metric scale you stole from McKinley High?"

Randy's eyes practically pop out of his head. "Dylan, are you totally whacked? Purple-bud in Mom's studio? A scale? I haven't even been in there since she left!"

Chloe walks over and kneels beside me. Her hair is tied up in that signature messy knot, and when the breeze blows I smell her perfume. She studies the back of my head, which is really throbbing now, then gently runs her fingers over my cheek. It wouldn't be a bad way to die. "Dylan, are you sure you're okay?" she says. "I mean, a lot of stuff has happened lately, with your mom leaving and all. Maybe you just need to talk about it. Get some things off your chest."

Moser chimes in. "Yeah, dude, in fact, I can give you the

name of this therapist my parents sent me to after they confiscated my computer because they thought I was obsessed with Kurt Cobain's suicide-slash-murder. Which we all know was a premeditated plot by the evil Courtney Love. Anyway, she was really nice, the therapist, I mean. Pretty, too."

Headbone throws up his hands. "Come on, Moser, Dylan doesn't need a shrink! He's got us!"

Randy picks up the basketball and throws it at Headbone. "Yeah, right. *Doctor* Headbone. What a joke."

Nick, who obviously doesn't like the fact that Chloe is tenderly stroking my face, crosses his arms over his chest and says, "I have an idea. Why don't we take a look? We can dig up Randy's stash in the backyard and then check out the studio. That way Dylan can see for himself that no one here is dealing drugs."

Randy shrugs. "Fine with me. What do you say, Dylan?"

At this point, I'm feeling pretty woozy and begin to think that maybe I *did* imagine the whole thing. "All right," I say, "I guess we can check it out."

While Nick, Chloe, and I accompany Randy to the burial spot in the backyard, Moser patrols the front of the house in case any cops drive by, or even worse, Mrs. Underwood happens to be walking her yappy runt poodle. Headbone's job is to keep his eyes peeled for old man Pellegrino.

"Here it is," Randy says. He's on his knees in the grass, holding out a wooden box caked with dirt. "Take a look for yourself, Dyl." Randy hands me the box and I open the lid. Inside is a sandwich-sized Ziploc bag containing a small amount of weed. Regular Colombian. "Like I said, that's about one ounce. Just enough for me and my buds for a few weeks, if they agree to return the favor."

"Hey, old man Pellegrino's curtains just shifted," Headbone says. "And there's a strange-looking nose poking out the window. I think he's spying on us."

We all look up. "Are you tripping, Headbone?" Randy says. "That's his golden retriever. Stop being so paranoid."

Chloe puts a hand on my shoulder. "Dylan, are you sure you want to check out the studio now? Because, well, if you're not up to it, we can always do it some other time."

I look into her eyes—light brown with a fringe of pale lashes. "No," I say. "I'm ready. Let's get it over with."

Randy buries the box, and we all go inside. Tripod follows as we climb the stairs and enter my mom's studio, and when Headbone accidentally bumps into him, he hisses, jumps up, and sinks his claws into Headbone's leg. "Ow! Hey, get off me!" Headbone grabs Tripod by the back of his neck and flings him out the door. "I told you we should have strung up that stupid cat after he chewed Dylan's goldfish! He's a bloody killer!"

The antique table is still where I left it, right next to the picture window. I push the table aside and see that the boards underneath are securely nailed down. I get on my hands and knees and run my fingers along the smooth surface. "What do you think, Dylan?" Randy says. "Could it have been a bad dream?"

"Yeah, that's it," Headbone says. "Although I must admit, finding a stash of purple-bud wouldn't exactly be *my* idea of a bad dream."

I ignore Headbone, and as I continue to run my hands over the boards, I discover that while most of the nailheads are old and dingy, a few are the color of a shiny new nickel. I look up; except for Nick, who's studying the floor intently, no one seems to notice. A second later, he and I lock eyes, and in that moment I can tell that Nick sees the shiny nailheads too. "Yeah," I say, deciding to keep our little secret for now. "You guys were right. It must have been a bad dream. Sorry for all the trouble."

"Hey, it's okay," Randy says. He hunkers down next to me and pats me on the back. "So, Dylan, have you had enough abuse for one day, or do you want to finish that game of one-on-one?"

I haven't looked at myself in the mirror yet, but if my face is anything like Randy's, it's not going to be pretty. "Um, how about we call it a draw?"

"Sounds good to me."

After Randy and I wash up, Chloe bandages our wounds, scolding us the entire time, and soon the Dead Musicians Society is back in the basement playing "Voodoo Child," with Chloe on keyboards and singing backup vocals. Meanwhile, I go to my room, take out my guitar, and begin to practice a piece by Carcassi, but the notes on the page are fuzzy and the staffs have way too many lines. So I give up, pop a few aspirin for my splitting headache, set my alarm for 8 a.m., and climb into bed.

The next thing I know, my father is shaking me. "Dylan, wake up! Are you all right?" The sun is pouring through the blinds, and my head feels like it's locked in a vise.

"Yeah, Dad, I'm okay, I guess." I glance at the clock and

see that it's already noon. I've slept through my alarm and missed our final AAU game. I try to sit up, but my ribs ache and my head pounds. I flop back down.

My dad pulls a miniature flashlight from the pocket of his scrubs, opens my right eyelid, and shines the light into my pupil. "Randy told me that the two of you got into a fight playing basketball. He said you hit your head pretty hard. I'm worried you might have a concussion, Dylan. How long have you been sleeping?"

"Um . . ." I do the math while he checks my left eye. "I don't know, Dad, maybe ten hours." It's actually been closer to fourteen, but I don't want him freaking out more than he already is. I can't believe I've missed the game. Coach Heffner is going to kill me.

My dad turns off the flashlight and slips it back into his pocket. "I think you're okay, but I'm going to have to keep a close watch on you for the next twenty-four hours. Turn around, let me check the back of your head." I do as he says. My whole body hurts. "I heard Chloe patched you guys up." He lifts the bandage and inspects underneath. "It looks like she did a pretty good job, but honestly, Dylan, why didn't you call me? I've already read Randy the riot act. I mean, really, this could have been serious."

"I don't know, Dad. I'm sorry. It's just . . . I thought I was okay. Besides, you said Labor and Delivery was a zoo."

"It doesn't matter how busy I am, Dylan, you can always call me. If anything's wrong, I'll be there. You know that."

"Yeah, Dad, I know." But the truth is since my mom left, the few times I've called my dad at work he's always been in the middle of some major gynecological emergency. "So, how's Randy?" I say.

He sighs. "Well, like you, he's got some contusions to the face. Also, his left eye is swollen shut, and his right elbow might need a few stitches. But other that that, I think he'll live."

"Oh." What I feel is a mixture of pride that I was able to hold my own in a fight against my older brother and a good measure of remorse for having started the whole thing, since I probably resemble Frankenstein at the moment and am soon going to get my ass chewed out by Coach Heffner.

"I just don't understand this, Dylan. You and your brother have always gotten along. When I asked Randy what had happened, he flat-out refused to tell me. What caused the fight?"

"Um, nothing really *caused* the fight, Dad. We were just playing some one-on-one and the game got out of control." From the look on his face, I can tell he's not buying this story. I sit up and grimace, trying not to moan.

"Here," he says, "let me examine the rest of you." With his stethoscope, he listens to my heart and lungs; then he runs his fingers over my sore ribs. "Well, you're pretty banged up, but nothing's broken, thank God."

We sit there for a while in silence. Lately my father has been looking pretty worn out, and today, if he wasn't wearing doctor's scrubs, you might mistake him for a homeless guy in need of a shave and a good meal. "I'm sorry for all the trouble, Dad," I say. "It won't happen again."

He takes a deep breath and exhales slowly. "Listen,

Dylan, I've been doing a lot of thinking lately, and I've reached the conclusion that we need some help around here. I'm going to start interviewing for a live-in housekeeper."

"What? No, Dad, you can't do that! Look, I've been doing a good job with the cooking and cleaning and stuff. I know the house isn't perfect, but—"

"No, Dylan, that's not it. Sure, you've been doing a great job, and I'm proud of you, but we need to face the facts. I don't know if you heard the phone message from Mom, but it seems that when she gets back from Paris, she's planning to stay in the Village. With Philippe."

It's the first time I've heard my dad say Philippe's name since my mother moved out. A burning knot forms in the back of my throat. "Is . . . that what she said? I only heard part of the message."

He nods. "I'm sorry, Dylan. I was hoping she'd reconsider, come back home, but it doesn't look like that's going to happen."

Suddenly I miss my mother more than ever. I can't even imagine some strange lady coming to our house—cooking, cleaning, trying to act like she gives a crap about some rich doctor's kids. A tear slides down my cheek and I quickly wipe it away. "Whatever, Dad, I still don't want a housekeeper. Randy and I can manage fine on our own."

He raises an eyebrow. "Well, considering that during this past week—let's see, you've been arrested, Mrs. Underwood called the cops on Randy, and then the two of you tried to kill each other, I'd say you guys need a little supervision. Besides, I work such crazy hours. There needs to be an adult around when I'm not here."

I'm about to protest again, but he stops me. "Shhh, we'll talk about this later, Dylan." He leans over and fluffs my pillow. "For now, just rest."

I sleep away the next couple of days, waking only to eat, watch *Seinfeld* reruns, read my old copy of *The Catcher in the Rye*, and think about Angie. By Labor Day, except for the fact that my face looks like it's been through a meat grinder, I'm feeling pretty good. Angie will be home this evening and, who knows, maybe if I put a bag over my head, I'll gain enough courage to tell her how I feel about her.

I get up, shower, put the finishing touches on my da Vinci sketch, which is due tomorrow in art class, and practice my guitar piece. After dinner, I sit by the phone waiting for Angie to call. She never does. Finally, at ten-thirty, I give in and dial her number. Her mom answers. "Hello?"

"Um, hi, Mrs. McCarthy, this is Dylan. Sorry to call so late. Is Angie home?"

"Oh, hi, Dylan. Actually, no, she's not here. Jonathan Reed stopped by earlier, and I believe they went to the movies. Can I take a message?" There's a long pause. "Dylan? Are you still there?"

"Oh . . . yes. I'm here. No, no message, but thanks anyway."

"Sure thing. I'll tell her you called."

I flop onto my bed and stare at the ceiling, wondering

why I haven't followed through with my original plan to rid the earth of Jonathan Reed. About twenty minutes later, as I'm plotting a new and even more sadistic murder, the phone rings. From the caller ID I see that it's Angie, but I don't pick up. When it rings again at eleven-fifteen, I put on one of my prized vintage LPs—the Beatles, *Sergeant Pepper's Lonely Hearts Club Band*—turn out the lights, and swear off girls forever.

Nine

AT SCHOOL THE NEXT DAY I make an effort to lie low, but as I'm heading to second-period class, I hear Angie's voice behind me in the hallway. "Dylan, wait up!" I turn around and see Jonathan Reed walking beside her. He looks the same—handsome in that Orlando Bloom–ish pretty-boy sort of way—only now he's making a fashion statement by wearing a pair of rectangular nerd-band glasses, popular with Weezer fans and guys on the debate team. Tucked under his arm is a copy of Hemingway's *A Moveable Feast*. How literary.

"Oh, my God!" Angie says when she sees me, clapping one hand over her mouth. "Dylan, what happened to your face?" One thing about Angie, she's never been subtle.

Since I'm not in the mood to explain, I say, "Um, nothing much."

Jonathan nods hello while I give him the once-over.

"What do you mean *nothing?*" Angie demands. "You're all beat up! You look terrible!"

"Thanks."

I turn and continue to class. "Dylan, wait, I need to talk to you!" Angie follows me, and unfortunately Jonathan tags along. "I called you twice last night," she says. "Why didn't you answer the phone?"

I shrug and keep walking. "I don't know. I was tired. I went to bed early."

"But I wanted to talk to you about the movie!"

Angie, who I've decided is the biggest narcissist on the planet, is referring to her all-important short film, but just to be a wiseass I say, "Oh, you mean the movie you two saw last night? How was it?"

Angie looks at Jonathan and rolls her eyes. "No, Dylan. The movie I'm *making*. The one you're starring in. Remember?"

"Ohhhhh, that one. Yeah, vaguely. What about it?" I slow down and come to a halt outside the fine arts room. I peer in and see my teacher, Mr. Wiseman, hunched over a drawing on his desk.

"Well," Angie says, ignoring my sarcasm, "I've been going over the footage all week, and when Jonathan stopped by last night I showed it to him. We had this intense brainstorming session, and we've come up with the most amazing idea!" Angie's eyes are wide with excitement. "Not only are you the star of my film, you're also the subject. It's kind of like *Being John Malkovich* with a slightly different twist. Anyway, I even have a title." She closes her eyes and takes a deep breath. *"The Latent Powers of Dylan Fontaine."*

Jonathan is grinning from ear to ear, and now that I've got a taste for blood, I have a sudden urge to punch him in the mouth. "Dylan," he says, "I've got to say, the scene in the park with that Australian juggling chain saws over you is, like, classic."

Jonathan has many irritating habits, one of them being his overuse of the word *classic*. "Well, Jonathan," I say, "I'm glad you found the whole thing entertaining, but"—I turn back to Angie—"sorry, I'm not doing it."

"What? No, Dylan, please, you have to!"

"Nope." The bell rings and Mr. Wiseman gets up from his chair. Students start pouring into his room.

Val Knudsen, sporting a new eyebrow ring and a shock of purple hair, gets a load of my face as she strolls into class. "Looking good, Fontaine," she says with a grin. "Didn't know you were such an animal."

"Dylan," Angie pleads. "Come on, you know how important this is to me. You can't say no!"

"Angie's right, Dylan," Jonathan chimes in. "The material she's got so far—you on the train, in the park—it's, like, magical."

The only magical thing I'm interested in right now is Jonathan Reed disappearing into thin air. Or, better yet, being sawed in two. "Angie," I say, "can I talk to you alone for a minute?"

"Oh, yeah, sure. Um . . . I'll see you later, Jonathan?"

For a guy who's supposedly a literary genius, Jonathan is

slow at catching on to plain English. "Oh . . . right. Later, Angie." He places one hand on my shoulder, which I deeply resent, and whispers in my ear, "Think about it, Dylan. It'll make a great short. Angie's counting on you."

When Jonathan is halfway down the hall I say to Angie, "My, that was a record-length breakup. What was it? Two and a half weeks?"

"Is that what you're angry about, Dylan? For your information, Jonathan and I are *not* together. We're just friends."

"Friends?" This is an interesting concept, considering Jonathan's recent philandering. "So what happened to Hannah Jaworski?"

Angie clears her throat and cracks a little smile. "She dumped him a few days ago. Apparently she's dating an older guy from Brooklyn College. Serves him right, huh?"

"Ahhhh, I see. Jonathan gets dumped, and then he comes crawling back to you. *Classic.*"

Angie gets my joke, but instead of laughing she makes a face. "No, Dylan, it's not like that at all. Jonathan came by my house last night to say he was sorry for being a jerk, and even though I've been angry and hurt and all that, I decided to do the mature thing and accept his apology. Anyway, after that we started talking and I showed him the film I was working on. He thought it was awesome and offered to help shoot it, so—"

"Whoa, whoa, wait a minute. I thought *I* was helping you."

"Well, you were, I mean, you *are.* It's just, I need someone else, since you're too close to the subject matter." She grins. "In other words, *you*. I want a more objective point of view. Jonathan's perfect for the job."

It figures that now that Mr. Cinematography has arrived, I have to take a backseat. I shake my head. "Look, Angie, I'm not your guinea pig, okay? And I'm not going to Washington Square Park with Jonathan Reed. I said I'd help you shoot the film, and yeah, I'd even be in it, but a story about the real *me* is not happening. Besides"—I hold out my arms—"what could possibly be so interesting?"

Her face lights up. "That's the whole point, Dylan! Nothing!"

"Wow, you're just full of compliments today, aren't you?"

I head for class, but Angie grabs my arm. "Wait, Dylan, please, I'm sorry, that's not what I meant."

Like a glutton for punishment, I stop and look into her eyes, which have this uncanny way of melting me in two seconds flat. "Okay, then what *did* you mean?"

"What I should have said, Dylan, is that there's so much inside you, but it's all locked up in here." She reaches over and taps my chest. "I want the movie to be an experimental piece about your life, and I think that's what'll make it great—stand out above the rest. I know I'm begging, but there's really no one else who can do it. Only you."

Somehow, I don't think Angie has quite redeemed herself. "Hmm," I say, "sounds to me like I'm the only person you know who's stupid enough to get filmed with a bunch of mental cases in New York City."

While Angie lets out an exasperated sigh, the late bell rings. Down the hall I see Randy and Nick turn the corner and stop outside their music theory class. A few seconds later Franz Warner joins them. "Wow," Angie says, "now I get it. That's why your face looks the way it does. You and Randy got into a fight, didn't you?"

I nod, watching the three of them, wondering if Franz Warner is also connected to the imaginary purple-bud in my mom's studio. They exchange a few words, and then Randy and Nick head into class.

"Well, it's about time you stood up to Randy," Angie goes on, "considering the fact that *you* got arrested because of *him*."

"Mr. Fontaine? Are you planning to join us today, or should I go ahead and mark you tardy?" Mr. Wiseman is standing in the doorway. His scruffy gray beard is poking out in all directions and there's a smudge of charcoal on his cheek.

"Listen, Angie, I gotta go. And about the movie, I'm sorry, but I can't—"

She places one finger over my mouth. "Dylan, don't decide now. Just take a little time and think about it, okay?"

Angie's so close I can smell the spearmint on her breath, and her finger pressed against my lips puts me in mind of things completely unrelated to short films and grumpy art teachers. I've already made my decision—I'm not going to help her with the film, not if Jonathan Reed is in the equation—but for now I say, "Fine, whatever, I'll think about it."

The only seat open in class is the one next to Val Knudsen, so I have no choice but to take it. As I slide into the chair, she unrolls a large sheet of paper and spreads it across her desk. It's filled with her usual amazing pen-and-ink drawings of werewolves, vampires, dragons, and other gothic creatures, some with swords piercing their hearts and dripping blood. When Mr. Wiseman makes his way around the room, checking out our summer projects, Val leans over and whispers, "Hey, Fontaine, seriously, what happened to your face?"

I pull out the cardboard tube that's holding my da Vinci drapery sketch. "Nothing. I got into a fight with my brother." Val hangs out with the alternative crowd, so even though she's just a sophomore, she's acquainted with the guys in the Dead Musicians Society.

"You got in a fight with Randy? Why?"

"Oh, lots of reasons. Mainly, I got arrested last week because of him. The cops found *his* weed in *my* pocket."

"Wow, heavy." She studies me for a while, then starts to grin. "So, how does Randy look?"

I crack a smile. "Not much better."

She nods. "Vengeance is sweet, isn't it?"

Mr. Wiseman pauses at Addie Myers's desk, admiring her depiction of the Brooklyn Bridge, then approaches Val and me. "Mr. Fontaine, are you planning to share your artwork with the class, or are you waiting for a special unveiling?"

"Oh, no, here it is." I open the tube and shake out its contents. As I unravel the paper, he looks on and begins to smile.

"Well, well, an old master sketch. Nicely done. Da Vinci would be honored."

I feel a warm surge of pleasure. Mr. Wiseman might be a crotchety old pain in the ass, but he's a very good artist and I value his opinion. "Thanks, Mr. Wiseman."

Val takes a look at my sketch and snorts.

"Is there a problem, Ms. Knudsen?" Mr. Wiseman says.

"Um . . . well." Val looks at me. "Yes, actually."

"Maybe you'd like to share your observations with the class. Mr. Fontaine, do you mind if Ms. Knudsen critiques your work?"

Before Val started drawing gothic fantasy creatures, she drew realistic landscapes and portraits that Mr. Wiseman called "unique and haunting." Everyone, including me, thought they were awesome. But after Val pierced her tongue and got the Chinese symbols for life and death tattooed on either side of her belly button, she became more cutting-edge. "Um . . ." I look at Val. "No, I don't mind."

"Okay, then, Ms. Knudsen," Mr. Wiseman says. "You may have the floor."

Mr. Wiseman takes a seat on an empty desk while Val clears her throat. Underneath the black eyeliner, piercings, and tattoos, Val is really quite soft. I can tell she's nervous. "Well," she says, "I understand why it's important to study the old masters, but I think Dylan is at a point in his artistic career where he should move on. You know, find his own style."

Great. First I have to listen to Angie tell me how non-spontaneous I am, and now Val announces that I have no style. Maybe the two of them should get together and critique my whole life.

Mr. Wiseman nods. "I see. In other words, the same way you did, Ms. Knudsen?" He peers over at Val's summer project. Although Mr. Wiseman is not one to squelch creativity, he is not a fan of *Dracula Slays the Evil Centaur.*

"Yes," Val says, defiantly. "The same way I did."

"Fair enough," Mr. Wiseman says. "Mr. Fontaine, Ms. Knudsen may have a valid point. It's certainly something to consider for your next project. Now, moving right along . . ."

While Mr. Wiseman hands out the semester syllabus, Val reaches over and touches my hand. "Sorry, Fontaine. Sometimes the truth hurts."

Ten

A STRANGE LADY IS STANDING at our kitchen sink washing dishes. She's built like a Mack truck, and to my horror she's singing "Goodnight, Irene" completely off-key in what I believe is a German accent. I open the refrigerator and grab an apple, wondering if my dad's classified ad for a housekeeper read: *Must like country music and Wiener schnitzel. Former woman wrestler a plus.*

I bite into the apple and she spins around. "Oh, hello! You must be Dylan!" Her face is round and pleasant, and it looks like she's been working hard, because the kitchen is spotless. She grabs a dish towel above the sink, revealing two large armpit stains. Hastily she dries her hands and offers me one. "So nice to meet you. I'm Vanya."

We shake. Her grip is firm and solid, like a man's. "Um, hi, Vanya. I guess you're our new . . . ," and that's when I see a jumble of raw multicolored sausage links on the counter—brown, white, and bloodred.

"Yes, yes, your new housekeeper. Your father asked me to come today. And maybe"—she smiles—"if we all get along, I will agree to stay."

"Oh, okay." I point to the counter. "What are those?"

"Why, that's our dinner! Bratwurst, *bierwurst,* and *weisswurst.* I found them all at the German deli on Third Avenue. For dessert, I'm making strudel. Tonight we'll have a feast. I've even invited your brother's friends to join us."

As I stand there gaping, Randy calls me from the top of the stairs. "Hey, Dyl, is that you?"

"Yeah, it's me. Um, listen, Vanya, I better go. Sounds like Randy needs me."

"Sure, sure. Run along, dinner is at six."

Vanya goes back to the sink while I trek up the stairs. Inside Randy's room I find the whole gang. Randy is sitting atop his desk, Moser and Headbone are sprawled out on the floor, and Nick and Chloe are lounging cozily on the bed. The five of them seem to be having a meeting.

"Dylan?" Randy says. "Did you know the Vagina Head was hiring a housekeeper?"

"Uh, well . . ." I look around. They're all staring at me like I'm some kind of traitor. "Yeah, sort of."

He throws up his hands. "Sort of? So why didn't you tell me? The guys and I cut out of school early to practice and— "

"Ahem!" Chloe says.

"Sorry, Clo. *The band and I* cut out of school early to

practice, and when we got here, there was this . . . this *lady*—"

Headbone chimes in. "And we're using that term loosely, dude. Did you see the size of her?"

Moser laughs. "Yeah. We already gave her a nickname. Attila the Hun."

Chloe takes off one of her flip-flops and throws it at Moser, hitting him in the back of the head. "You'd better watch it, Moser, or I'm going to drag your sorry butt into the shower and scrub you down with Betadine."

"Ouch!" Moser says, rubbing his head. "Jeez, Clo, it was just a joke."

"Okay, okay," Randy says. "Anyway, Dyl, this lady, whatever her name is, *Vanya,* starts going off on us about how she's planning to call the school and let them know we skipped class. Then she told us there's not going to be any more monkey business around here—she actually used that term, *monkey business*—and that we couldn't play our music until four-thirty, when the school day was technically over."

"And . . . you guys listened to her?" I say.

Headbone sits up. "What were we supposed to do? She's a brute! Did you see those sausages in the kitchen? She probably slaughtered the pig herself! Seriously, what was your dad thinking when he hired her? I mean, what does he really know about her background? She could be a freaking Nazi. A skinhead!"

Nick leans over, slips off Chloe's other flip-flop, and flings it at Headbone. "Get a grip, Headbone. We all want to get rid of Vanya, but she's no skinhead."

"Whatever," Headbone says.

While the guys brood, I gather up the flip-flops, hand them to Chloe, and take a seat on the bed next to her. Suddenly Moser blurts out, "Hey, I have an idea! How about we *all* stop showering? Think about it, guys, Vanya wouldn't be able to take it. She'd *have* to quit!"

Everyone except Moser groans. "Sorry, Moser," Nick says, slipping his arm around Chloe, "some of us actually have a *reason* to smell good." He nuzzles her neck and she begins to giggle. I raise an eyebrow at Randy. He frowns and looks away.

"Hey, I got a better idea," Headbone says. "Let's see if we can bribe her with some weed. I mean, she's German, right? And Germany is right next to Austria, where pot's legal. I'm telling you, those Europeans are, like, *far out* when it comes to drugs. Vanya's probably been smoking since she was a kid."

"You know, Headbone," Randy says, "for a guy who's supposedly Harvard material, you've got the common sense of an orangutan."

Headbone smiles. "Thanks, dude."

Moser shakes his head. "Hey, Randy, when's your mom coming back? I mean, yeah, she used to read us the riot act and kick us out of the house if she smelled reefer, but at least she was your *mom*. Headbone's right, who *is* this lady?"

Suddenly the room goes silent. Headbone gives Moser a shove and whispers, "Foot in mouth!"

"Oh, sorry, Randy," Moser says. "Really, I didn't mean anything, I just . . ."

Randy shakes his head. "No, it's all right, Moser." He looks at me. "Hey, Dyl, can I talk to you for a minute? Alone?"

"Yeah, sure." I hop off the bed, and while the others look on with concerned expressions, the two of us walk into the hall. Randy shuts the door. "Listen," he says. "Did Dad say anything to you about Mom coming home?"

I look into Randy's eyes, and I can tell that he misses our mother as much as I do. Maybe more. Our parents have always tried not to play favorites, but the truth is, while my dad has a natural affinity for me, I think my mother has always felt more connected to Randy. Probably because they're so much alike. "Well . . ." I hesitate.

"Dylan, just tell me. I need to know."

"Okay. Yeah, Dad talked to me. He told me she's not coming home. When she gets back from Paris, she'll still be living with Philippe in the Village."

Randy leans against the wall, then slides down until he's sitting, hunched over, his knees against his chest. He stares straight ahead. I sit next to him and very gently place my hand on his back. I'm expecting him to shrug it off, but he doesn't. "It sucks," I say. "The whole thing. It just sucks."

He nods. "I just . . . I don't understand why, you know? I mean, it's not like Dad's a bad guy or anything. Yeah, they used to fight a lot, and sure, he was never around much, but he's got a tough job. Mom *knows* he loves her. And anyway, what about *us*?"

I think back to the last huge argument my parents had. It was the night of Philippe's art show. My mom had a few of her pieces on display, and she was very excited. We waited and waited, but my dad never came. There was no emergency at the hospital; we found out later he was making some last-minute phone calls and lost track of time. After that my mom began spending more time with Philippe and her friends in the Village. When she finally left, she cried a lot, hugged Randy and me, told us how much she loved us and that she needed time to think. Not once did she bad-mouth my father. But still, for Randy and me it was the ultimate betrayal, and when my mom would call, sounding happy with her new-and-improved life, I spoke to her in monosyllables. Randy wouldn't even get on the phone. It was our form of revenge.

Slowly I run my hand up and down Randy's back, and he still doesn't shrug it off. "Yeah, I know what you mean, Randy. I miss Mom. A lot."

We sit there for a while in silence. Finally, Randy takes a deep breath and looks at me. His eyes are glassy, and it's not from smoking weed. "Well, I guess it's just you and me, huh, Dyl? And the Vagina Head, whenever he decides to show up."

I smile sadly. "Don't forget Attila the Hun."

"Oh, right, thanks for reminding me."

At the dinner table Vanya asks all six of us to hold hands, and just as she's about to say grace, Headbone pipes up. "Hey, wait a minute!" We all look at him. He slams a fist on the table. "What are you guys doing? This totally goes against the Dead Musicians Society's principles! I mean, what happened to our belief that religion is the opium of the masses? I don't think we should be forced to participate in—" Suddenly Headbone stops his tirade. Across the table, Vanya is glaring at him. "Oh, sorry, Vanya, it's just—"

"Well, Arthur," she says, "I think this would be a perfect opportunity for *you* to say the blessing."

Moser laughs. "Yeah, great idea, Vanya! Go for it, Headbone!"

The rest of us smile and nod our approval, and as we bow our heads we keep one eye on Headbone. He scowls, fidgets in his chair, and finally gives in. Closing both eyes, he says, "All right, *God,* if you're actually, you know, *up there,* please bless this"—he glances suspiciously at the multicolored sausages—"*fine dinner* we are about to eat. Amen."

Vanya opens her eyes and smiles wide. "Wonderful prayer, Arthur! Thank you! Now, let's dig in!"

Vanya passes around platters of food, making sure we all take at least one of her wienerwursts, but since you never know what's lurking inside one of those things (e.g., pig intestines, pig blood), when she's not looking I slip mine to Tripod, who is strategically perched by my foot under the table. Happily, I fill up on side dishes, and after making sure there is no lard or trans fat in the strudel, I have a large piece along with some vanilla ice cream. Afterward, we all thank Vanya for dinner, and while Chloe helps with the dishes, the guys go downstairs to practice. I head to my room.

Before taking out my prized cocobolo rosewood classical guitar, I consider giving Angie a call to tell her that maybe, just *maybe*, I'll consider being her guinea pig for her short film. But then I picture Jonathan Reed saying, "Lights, camera, action!" and change my mind. Instead, I open my drawer and pull out the photos of Angie and me, and, since there's no use hiding them anymore, I stick our favorite one—the two of us with Tony the goldfish—to my bedroom mirror. Then I begin. I play my Carcassi piece a few times, and about halfway through a piece by Fernando Sor, Chloe walks into my room. Immediately I stop plucking, but she motions for me to continue and takes a seat on my bed.

Now, what most people don't understand about playing classical guitar is that tension is the enemy. For your music to flow, you have to be completely relaxed—a difficult feat when a beautiful girl is sitting just a few feet away from you on your bed. So, after a few unfortunate twangs, I manage to get ahold of myself and finish the piece fairly well. When I'm done, Chloe smiles. "That was beautiful, Dylan. I had no idea you could play like that."

"Thanks." I rest the guitar on my lap. "Actually, I can do better. I was a little nervous with you in the room."

"Oh, well, just pretend I'm not here. In fact, I'll hide." Chloe makes an attempt to disappear by lying on her side with her back toward me, but it doesn't work. She's wearing a halter top, and her exposed back and shoulders are nice to look at. "Go ahead, Dylan," she says, talking to the wall, "please, keep playing."

Since I know the Sor piece by heart, I close my eyes and begin to play, and pretty soon I'm feeling the colors of the notes. I know it sounds a little Zen, but after a while I get lost in them. When I finish, I open my eyes and Chloe is standing beside me. "Awesome," she says, holding out both hands. "May I?"

"Oh, sure." I get up, offer Chloe my seat, and hand her the guitar. She holds it like it's made of glass.

"This is a beautiful instrument, Dylan." She plucks a few strings, listening carefully to the sound. "Will you show me how? I play a little acoustic."

"Okay." I stand behind the chair, lean over Chloe's bare shoulder, and show her how to hold the neck, where to place her hands, and how to pluck the strings with the tips of her fingernails.

After a brief lesson, she turns around. "Thank you, Dylan." She hands me back the guitar and takes a seat on the bed. I sit next to her. "So how'd you learn to play?"

"Oh, my friend Jake got me into classical. I take lessons from his instructor now, but Randy's the one who taught me to play guitar."

"Really? So I guess you guys used to be close, huh?"

I think back to when Randy first taught me on electric. No matter how bad I sucked, he always told me that I had talent and all I needed to do was practice. It still amazes me how patient he was. "Yeah, we hung out a lot together before he joined the band. Before he started getting high all the time." I look at Chloe and smile sadly. "Would you believe it? Randy even taught me to play basketball."

"Not surprising," she says, running a finger across my bruised cheek. "I had a feeling that was a love-hate game of one-on-one. You know, I've been talking to the guys about laying off the weed. I used to smoke a lot too, but I quit when I saw how it affected my music. Pot takes away your motivation. Ruins relationships, too."

We're quiet for a while, and soon Chloe sees the photo of Angie and me taped to the mirror. "Wow, that's great picture," she says. "So what's been going on with you and Angie?"

"Oh, nothing much." I try to sound blasé, but I feel my face getting hot. "I'm supposed to be helping her shoot this film in Washington Square Park, only now she's decided the movie is about *me,* so in order to be more objective, she wants to bring along her ex-boyfriend, Jonathan. Who, basically, is an asshole."

I expect Chloe to laugh, but she doesn't. "Sounds to me like you have some pretty strong feelings for Angie."

I blink a few times. "Well, I don't know, I mean—"

"I can tell," Chloe says. "I'm not psychic or anything, but it's a gift. Besides, your face kind of gives it away."

Fabulous.

"Listen, Dylan, take my advice. Don't let Jonathan get to you. Jealousy is a weakness. Girls don't like it."

I look into Chloe's eyes. At last I'm getting some insight into the female mind. "Hey, Chloe, can I ask you something?"

"Sure."

"Are you and Nick, like . . . together?"

"Ah, Nick. Yeah, more or less. Why?"

"Well, when I first met you, I thought you and Randy might hook up. You must have figured out he likes you."

Chloe is quiet for a long time. Finally, she says, "Has . . . Randy ever *said* anything to you about me? You know, in that way?"

"Well, no, but that's just Randy. Believe me, I can tell. He's crazy about you."

Chloe stares out the bedroom window. "Dylan, I know you don't think much of Nick, but he and I are a lot alike. We both want the same things—to make it big, be famous one day. Your brother is different. Special. He doesn't care about any of that, he just loves the music. The other night I heard his original stuff, and it blew me away. I told him he should keep writing, that he's got a gift. Anyway, if he and I ever got close, I'd disappoint him."

"No," I say. "That's not true. You'd never disappoint him."

Chloe shrugs and lowers her eyes. From the look on her face I can tell she doesn't want to talk about this anymore.

"Chloe?" I say. "Can I ask you one more question? It's kind of important."

"Sure, Dylan. What is it?"

"The weed, under the floorboards in the studio. Do you believe that I saw it?"

She nods slowly. "Yeah, I do. But I don't know how it got there, and I don't know how it disappeared. That's a mystery."

"Okay, but . . . any ideas?"

She ponders this for a moment. "I don't think any of the guys are stupid enough to deal, and since no one's owning up, I hope it was a one-time mistake that'll never happen again."

"Hmm, I hope you're right."

"Now." She points to my guitar. "Will you play me another piece?"

"Sure." I take a seat in the chair, and Chloe lies down again with her back facing me. After a few pieces I notice that her breathing is slow and steady. I set down my guitar, and when I see that she's asleep I go to cover her with a sheet, but then I stop. Instead, I grab a stick of charcoal, open my sketchbook, sit down, and begin to draw the lines of her back with quick, loose strokes. When I finish the sketch I rip out the sheet, ready to do another, but the noise wakes Chloe. "Dylan?" she says. She sees the charcoal and paper. "Oh . . ."

"I'm sorry," I say, "it's just . . . you looked so beautiful, and I—"

"Wait," she says. "Here, try this." To my surprise, she slides off her halter top and lowers her jeans, arranging the sheet so that I can see the full curve of her back, the rise of her hip, and the slightest swell of her breast. "That's better," she says.

"Yeah," I agree. "It sure is."

Eleven

THAT EVENING, while Chloe falls asleep on my bed, I sketch her long, beautiful, seminaked body from multiple angles in all sorts of media—charcoal, pencil, conté crayon, and pen and ink. I even incorporate what I learned from my da Vinci drapery sketch and draw the ruffled sheet surrounding her with lots of depth and shadow. By midnight I'm exhausted, so I throw a sleeping bag onto the floor and pass out on top of it. When I wake in the morning, the bed is empty, the shower is running, and Randy is sitting at my desk, flipping though my sketches.

"Dylan, these drawings, they're . . . incredible," he says.

I sit up and rub my eyes. "Thanks. Um, what's going on? Is that Chloe in the shower?"

"Yep. She slept here last night. In your bed. But I guess you already know that." He gives me a wry smile. "Tell me, dude. How'd you do it? How'd you get her to pose nude for you?"

"Oh, come on, Randy," I say. "Chloe didn't pose *nude*. She just kind of slipped off her top and arranged the sheet so I could get a few interesting sketches for art class."

"A few *interesting* sketches, huh? I'll say. Wiseman's gonna be in art-teacher heaven." He holds up one of the pen-and-ink drawings and takes a closer look. "Listen, Dyl, do yourself a favor. Don't let Nick see these. He'll *freak*."

A grin spreads across my face as I imagine Nick flipping through my erotic drawings of Chloe. "Actually," I say, "I was planning to tape a few to the refrigerator. Maybe even slip one into a box of Pop-Tarts."

Randy looks up. "I'm serious, man. He'll *kill* you."

"I'm just kidding. Nick won't lay eyes on them."

The shower stops, and from the bathroom I hear Chloe singing Janis Joplin's "I Need a Man to Love." I try not to imagine her toweling off, which is almost impossible, and do my best to focus on Randy, who's studying my sketches and practically salivating. "Hey, Randy," I say. "Before Chloe comes back I need to tell you a few things."

He glances up from a sketch. "Oh, yeah, what?"

"Well . . ." I stand up, take the drawings from his hand, and set them on the desk. "Last night before she fell asleep we started talking, and she told me how she feels about you."

"Feels? About . . . *me?*"

"Yeah. When I mentioned your name she got all sad and serious. She said that you're a very *special* person, and that if the two of you ever hooked up, she'd only disappoint you."

"What?" Randy looks at me like I'm crazy. "What's *that* supposed to mean?"

"I don't know. Pretty insane, huh? It's like she couldn't have *you* so she settled for *Nick*. She says the two of them are more alike—they both want to make it big. Be famous one day."

"More alike?" Randy stands up, runs his fingers through his hair, and starts pacing the floor. "That *is* insane. Chloe and Nick are about as different as you can get."

From the bathroom I hear Chloe turn the doorknob. "Hey! I'm standing here dripping wet! Can one of you guys bring me a towel?"

I grin. "She's all yours, dude."

He makes a face at me, then calls back, "Yeah, sure, Chloe. Hold on, I'll be right there. Listen, Dyl, Chloe's with Nick. I've already accepted that. Besides, he's my best friend. I would never do that to him."

He grabs a towel that's draped over my chair, and just as he's about to head out the door, I say, "Randy, wait." He turns around. "Before you swear allegiance to your buddy Nick, let me ask you one question. Did *he* ever consider how *you* felt before swooping in on the girl of your dreams? I don't think so."

He shakes his head. "There are a lot of things you don't understand, Dylan. And besides, this is none of your business. Stay out of it."

"All right, but the way I see it, you've got nothing to lose. Last time I checked, the Dead Musicians Society didn't allow girls to come between their members. Even Nick swore that oath. True blue to the end."

Randy stands in the doorway, watching me. "Yeah, but there's a big difference. Chloe's part of the band."

I shrug. "Minor technicality."

"Hey! What do I have to do to get a towel around here?" Chloe shouts. "Run through the hallway naked?"

"Keep your shorts on, Clo!" Randy says. "Oh, but I forgot. You don't *have* any shorts." The two of us laugh.

"Har, har," Chloe calls from the bathroom. "You guys are a regular riot. Now. Bring. Me. The. Towel."

I raise an eyebrow at Randy. "It's your choice, bro. But I say go for it."

After playing Cupid, I roll up the sketches of Chloe and slip them into my trusty cardboard tube, wondering what Val and Mr. Wiseman are going to say about my new and improved artistic style: seminaked girls.

"Well, well, Mr. Fontaine, looks like you've been busy." It's second period and Mr. Wiseman is behind me, breathing down my neck and gazing at the sketches spread across my desk. "Hmm, *excellent* job. Your strokes are loose and fluid— I like that. And your subject, well . . ." Mr. Wiseman seems to be at a loss for words. "I must say, your subject *is* intriguing."

Val is sitting next to me, gawking. "Jeez, Fontaine!" She picks up one of the sketches and studies it. "I can't believe you did this! It's great!"

By now, everyone in class is surrounding my desk, trying to get a better look.

Val nudges me. "So who is she? Anyone I know?"

Val probably knows who Chloe is, since she goes to our school, so I need to be discreet. "Maybe," I say. "Or . . . maybe not."

Val grins. "I get it. You don't want to say. That's cool."

"Okay, everyone." Mr. Wiseman claps his hands a few times. "Settle down and take your seats. Today we'll begin sketching graphite portraits. Select a partner—someone you'd like to draw—and begin by framing his or her face. I'll be walking around the room if anyone needs help."

While people choose partners, Val stares down at her desk. Last year when we drew portraits, she sketched Mary Flannery with a knife in her throat and one bloody eyeball hanging out of its socket. It didn't go over well. "Hey, Val," I say, noticing that everyone is avoiding her like the plague, "you want to partner up?"

She glances at me shyly. "Um, are you sure about that, Fontaine? You might wind up looking like a freak."

I shrug. "You never know, it might be an improvement."

"Well"—she studies me for a moment—"all right, but I'm telling you right now, I don't pose nude."

When I've finished framing Val's face, I pencil in a hoop where her eyebrow ring will be, and then I get an idea. Instead of your standard carbon-copy portrait, I decide to try something a little different. Behind Val's face, like a ghosted-in background, I lightly sketch the silhouette of a girl with her arms outstretched. In her left hand I draw the Chinese symbol for life, and in the right, the symbol for death. "Hey, Val?" I say.

"Yeah?" She looks up from her paper.

"Thanks, you know, for giving me a kick in the ass—challenging me to try something new. I needed it."

"Anytime, Fontaine."

That night, before going to bed, I take my best drawing of Chloe, walk into my mom's studio, and tape it right next to my wine, avocado, and cheese still life. For the first time, I realize I've created something in the same league as Randy's. And it's not just because I had a beautiful, sexy model to work with, although of course that helped. My drawing is good, *really* good—with that quality Mr. Wiseman calls "emotional resonance." Anyway, the best part is that if you look very closely, in the right-hand corner of the drawing, hidden inside Chloe's pinky toe, are my initials. D.F. Dylan Fontaine.

"Dylan! Time for dinner!"

Surprisingly, it's my dad, not Vanya, calling me from the kitchen. Ever since Randy and I almost killed each other on the basketball court, he's been making a conscious effort to be home a few hours in the evening—share a meal with his sons like we're some kind of normal family.

"Coming!" I grab my guitar and head downstairs. After dinner I'm off to the Beanery. Jake calls it our weekly gig, but he's a little deluded. Mostly we sip overpriced chai lattes with a group of guys Headbone calls the Nerd Posse, play our latest pieces, and afterward talk about how much we suck.

The table is set for three, but Randy's not home. Ever

since my dad's been making these nightly appearances, Randy's been purposely absent. I can already see the look of disappointment on my dad's face. "So your brother's not here?"

"No, Dad, I, uh, think he's at Moser's."

"We'll save him a plate, Dr. Fontaine," Vanya says. "No need to worry."

My dad sighs and takes a seat. In an effort to be cheerful, he says, "Well, I'm glad you're here, Dylan. And Vanya, this smells wonderful."

I'm still wary of Vanya's cooking, but tonight she's prepared her German specialty—roast pork and sauerkraut— with peach cobbler for dessert. As I'm stuffing my face, my dad is chewing thoughtfully. "So how's school going?" he asks.

"Fine." I shove a forkful of food into my mouth.

"That's it? Fine?"

I swallow. "Well, yeah. What do you want me to say?"

"I don't know. Expound a little."

"Um . . ." I honestly can't think of anything unusual or exciting that happened in school. Well, except for the unveiling of my seminude sketches of Chloe, but I'm not about to share that with my father. "I don't know, Dad, my day was pretty boring. How was yours?"

He takes a bite of sauerkraut and thinks for a moment. "Boring too, I guess."   ·

The rest of the meal passes in silence, but as we're eating dessert, my dad pipes up, "Hey, the Yankees are playing tonight. You want to watch the game with me?"

"Oh, well, I'd like to, Dad, but it's Thursday. Jake and I have our gig at the Beanery."

"Oh, yeah, right. Well, maybe next time."

"Sure," I say. "Next time."

When I arrive, the guys are setting up to play, but as I'm about to join them, I see a strange banner hanging from the ceiling. The words are cut from white poster board and sprinkled with gold glitter. It reads THE LATENT POWERS OF DYLAN FONTAINE.

I stand there gaping, and a moment later the front door swings open. Headbone walks in. "Dylan! Why didn't you tell us you were the star of Angie's new film? We just found out you're doing a shoot here tonight. That's big news!" Following behind him is the rest of the band. Chloe, too. They take seats at a table.

I turn around. "Jake? What's going on?"

"I don't know," he says. "I was going to ask you the same question. When the guys and I got here, that sign was up. We thought it was some kind of a joke. What's it mean?"

Doug, the owner of the place, is watching us from behind the counter and chuckling. I guess he's in on the joke too. I shake my head. "It's Angie—she's making this stupid movie about me and . . . oh, forget it, I'll explain later. Have you seen her? Or that asshole Jonathan Reed?" But before Jake has a chance to answer, the two culprits walk through the door. Angie turns on her camera and starts to shoot. I march up to her and point my finger right at the lens. "This *isn't* funny, Angie. Put the camera away. *Now*."

She sighs, hits the Off button, and hands it to Jonathan. I stare him down until he walks away. "Chill *out*, Dylan," Angie says. "I just want to get a little background information before we do another shoot in the Village. Kind of like a prologue to the story."

I throw up my hands. "What are you talking about? What *story*? Look, Angie, I don't know what you're doing, but this is *not* cool, okay? Besides, I didn't even agree to do this film—"

"But Dylan, look around! You've got fans! If you back out now there's going to be a lot of disappointed people here, believe me."

"Angie, the only *fans* here are my brother, his burned-out friends, and the Nerd Posse."

"Um . . . you forgot Jonathan."

Jonathan is in the corner of the room, setting up a tripod. He looks up and gives me an enthusiastic smile.

I roll my eyes and mumble, "Oh, right, how could I forget? Mr. Cinematography."

"And me too, Dylan," Angie says, "your best friend *and* biggest fan. Now, please?" She waves me on. "Play a song. I'll get some musical footage, and then we'll start the interviews. Jonathan? Are you almost ready?"

Just as I'm about to rip down Angie's stupid banner and tell everyone to go home, I see Chloe, wagging her finger. I walk over. "Hey, Chloe. What's up?"

"Dylan, I think you should do the film. I mean, how

many people get this kind of chance? It could be a real adventure."

"I don't know, Chloe, I—"

"Just forget about everyone. Close your eyes and play, like you did for me the other night. Angie's really excited about this. And she's crazy about *you*. I can tell."

"Yeah, crazy, maybe. That's about it."

"Go on." She gives me a little push.

Reluctantly I head back, pick up my guitar, and take a seat with the guys. Jake leans over and whispers, "Dylan, this is great! Tonight we actually have an audience. *And* we're getting filmed." The Nerd Posse is nodding and grinning like it's their big night. I guess I can't disappoint them. I sigh and tune up my instrument, and soon the guys and I are taking turns playing our latest pieces. I run through my Sor study and my Carcassi piece, which surprisingly doesn't suck, and as the audience applauds I open my eyes and see Angie standing beside an empty chair in the middle of the room. Jonathan's got the camera rolling.

"Come, have a seat, Dylan," she says. Angie's dressed in black and her hair is curled into these long copper ringlets. She looks really pretty. Slowly I walk over. The room grows eerily quiet, and when I sit down I suddenly feel like I've been sentenced to the electric chair.

Twelve

ANGIE CLEARS HER THROAT and says, "Hi, everyone. Thanks for coming. Most of you know that I'm shooting a short film. It's an experimental piece, and Dylan is both my lead actor *and* the subject of the story. The screening, which I hope you'll all come to, will be in early November at NYU. Tonight I'll be going around asking questions, getting some information together." She turns to me and grins. "There's no script. So beware, Dylan, *anything* can happen."

At the nearby table, Headbone pipes up. "Wow, Dyl, this is *so* cool! Can I get a body autograph?" He stands, pulls a felt pen from his pocket, and hikes up his shirt. A huge mistake, seeing that Headbone's idea of a six-pack is sitting at the bottom of my dad's liquor cabinet labeled HEINEKEN. Headbone could also use a bra, and without a trace of embarrassment he points to a spot above his left boob. "Right here's perfect."

Before I can tell Headbone to shut up, Chloe yanks him back into his chair and Angie shoots him a warning look. "Okay, I think we're ready to begin," she says. "Doug? Will you bring Dylan a chai latte, on the house? Venti. And I believe he prefers soy milk. Now, Headbone, since you're so eager to talk, we'll start with you."

While Doug brings me one of his overpriced drinks, mumbling about how nice it would be to actually have some *paying* customers, Angie pulls out a small notebook and takes a seat across from Headbone. "So, Headbone, you've known Dylan for quite a long time, right?"

Headbone nods and flashes me a goofy grin. "Yep. Dylan's my bud. We're tight."

"Okay, great. How would you describe him?"

Angie should know better than to ask Headbone a vague, open-ended question. "Hmmm," Headbone says, "let's see. . . ." While the idiot stares up at the ceiling, I peer more closely at him, wondering if he's high. In my experience, the more weed he's smoked, the more he'll talk. Finally he says, "Dylan is . . . neat."

"Neat?" Angie says. "As in cool, groovy, neat-*o?*"

Headbone shakes his head. "No, no. Neat as in *clean.* Orderly. He likes to dust, vacuum, put things away." He laughs a little. "The rest of us"—he glances at Chloe—"oh, excuse me, Clo, *the guys in the band* are slobs, so it's one of those mutually agreed-upon, you know, symbiotic relationships."

If this is Headbone's epic description of me, it appears that he may actually *need* a few hits. Angie jots something in her book. "Um, can you give me a specific example of how Dylan is orderly?"

He shrugs. "Yeah, sure, that's easy. Dylan's got this really far-out collection of vintage LPs. Which is very cool, but he keeps them in"—he pauses and lowers his voice to a whisper—"alphabetical order."

I hear a few chuckles from the Nerd Posse. Angie and the band already know this embarrassing fact about me, but it would have been nice to keep it a secret from everyone else. While Angie scribbles in her book, I take a long drink of my chai latte and concentrate on burning a hole through Headbone's head with my laser-beam eyes. "Anything else you'd like to add?" Angie says.

Headbone thinks for a moment. "Nah, that's about it."

Unbelievable.

"Hold on, dude!" Moser says. "You're forgetting something *very* important!" He looks at Angie like he's had this major epiphany. "Dylan can cook! I'm telling you, that guy makes a *tasty* vegetable lasagna. Oh, and he's an excellent shopper. Reads *all* the labels. Won't allow anything artificial to pass his lips. Or ours. Especially yellow number 5. That stuff shrinks your balls." Everyone except me laughs. "Hey, it's true!" Moser says.

"All right, all right," Angie says with a sigh. "We've got neat, orderly, good cook, good shopper. Anything else, Moser?"

Moser scratches his head. "Um, no. Not at the moment."

It's amazing, the things I have to put up with.

Suddenly, Nick, who's been pretty distracted this whole time with peering out the window, pipes up. "Listen, Angie, you're wasting your time interviewing these two clowns. Just ask *me* a few questions, and maybe we'll get somewhere." He sits back, all cocky, like he's suddenly the Dylan Fontaine expert.

"Okay," Angie says. "Nick, how would you describe Dylan?"

Now, *this* should be interesting. Let's see what the snake in the grass has to say. "Well, the way I see it," Nick goes on, "Dylan's an all-around good guy. I mean, yeah, he's kind of straitlaced, and he can be obsessive about food and his LPs, but he's cool. Also, I hadn't heard him play in a while, but after tonight I'd say he's an *excellent* classical guitarist."

For the first time in my life I feel a strong sense of appreciation for Nick. Maybe he's not so bad after all. As Angie takes notes, he adds, "Oh, one more thing. Dylan can *draw*. He's done a lot of nice pieces, but that old master sketch he worked on this summer is really good."

Uh-oh, I think. Did Nick *have* to mention my artwork? I glance at Chloe. She elbows Randy. I try to stifle my laughter, but pretty soon all three of us are cracking up. "What?" Nick says. "What's so funny?"

Chloe reaches over and pats Nick on the head. "Nothing, Nick. Chill."

Headbone rolls his eyes like he's in on the joke, even though he's completely clueless. "Ah, forget it, Nick. Moser probably farted. What else is new?"

"Hey, I did not!" Moser says. "Jeez, Headbone, why do you always blame stuff on *me?*"

Angie shoots Moser and Headbone another warning look. "Okay, moving right along." She glances around the table until her eyes land on Chloe. "Chloe? What would you like to say about Dylan?"

From the corner, Jonathan hits the zoom button for a close-up. Meanwhile, I wait in eager expectation, hoping Chloe will begin by listing all my wonderful attributes, including my fabulous taste in music and what an excellent kisser I am. But instead, she purses her lips, draws her eyebrows together, and seems, well, confused. "I . . . haven't known Dylan very long," she says. "He's kind and thoughtful and sort of shy, but . . ." She glances at me with a sad, apologetic smile. "He's also insecure and has a hard time expressing his feelings. He's angry, too—about a lot of things."

The room grows quiet. A huge knot is forming inside my throat. I swallow and stare down at my feet while Angie scribbles in her book. I figure she's going to ask Randy a few questions next, but instead, she gets up, touches my shoulder as she passes by, and takes a seat beside Jake.

"Jake? You and Dylan have been friends for a long time. How would you describe him?"

"Oh, Dylan's a great guy. A friend you can always count on. And as far as talent goes, besides guitar, he's the best forward on our AAU team. He's got a real good chance of making varsity this year."

I cringe, grateful for the kudos, but did Jake *have* to mention varsity?

He's about to continue, but Headbone interrupts. "Um, Jake, dude, with all due respect, I have to disagree. I mean, yeah, for the most part Dylan's a loyal guy, but we've seen him play some pretty dirty basketball. Pushing, shoving, flagrant fouls, stuff like that." He jabs his thumb in Randy's direction. "Practically killed his own brother. Just ask Randy, he'll tell you."

Angie gives me a tentative glance. Slowly she walks over and takes a seat with the band. "Randy? Is . . . that true? Does Dylan play dirty basketball?"

Randy and I stare at each other. I can tell right away he's straight. "No, Dylan doesn't usually play dirty. But he *did* lose it that day we played a game of one-on-one. The truth is he's been acting pretty crazy lately. I'm not sure what his problem is, but like Chloe said, he's angry. Mostly with me. Seems to think I'm wasting my time playing with the Dead Musicians Society. But what my brother doesn't understand is that my first commitment is to the band." He pauses while Angie jots something in her book. "Also, Dylan seems to be *seeing* things lately—things that aren't really there."

Angie looks up, puzzled. I realize I haven't told her about the weed under the floorboards.

"And one more thing," Randy says. "I'm sorry you got arrested, Dylan. Really. It should have been me."

You could hear a pin drop. Angie sets down her pen and comes over to me. She whispers, "Dylan, I'm sorry. I didn't mean for this to get so intense. Maybe we should stop now."

Before I can answer, there's a rap on the coffee shop

window. A second later, Franz Warner walks in. He motions for Randy and Nick to follow him outside, but Nick shakes his head and pulls up a chair. Franz sits down.

"No, Angie, keep shooting," I say, glaring at Franz. "It's my turn to talk now."

"But . . . ," Angie says. "Are you sure?"

"Yeah, I'm positive." I motion for Jonathan to continue and fix my eyes on Randy. "You're absolutely right, Randy," I say. "I *have* been acting crazy lately. But you forgot to mention one *very* important thing. After Mom left us, and Dad checked out, and you started getting stoned every day of your sorry life, it's like I had no one. So yeah, maybe a person *can* start seeing things. In fact, maybe a person can lose his *mind*."

I glance around the room. Everyone's eyes are on me. "Oh, and the other thing Randy didn't mention," I add, "is that *he's* the real artist, and the best musician I know. Most of you have only heard the cover songs he does with the band, but before that he used to write his own music. His own lyrics, too. Really great stuff. I only wish I had a fraction of his talent. I know one thing—if I did, I'd never waste it."

Randy's glaring at me now. Chloe reaches over and puts a hand on his shoulder. He doesn't move. "Go ahead," I say to Angie. "See if he has anything left to say."

I can tell Angie doesn't want to do this. She takes a deep breath. "Um . . . Randy? Anything else?"

He nods slowly. "Yeah. Dylan needs to stop putting me on a pedestal. The truth is I'm *not* that good, bro. There are millions of talented people out there, and guess what? I'm not one of them. So stop looking to me for answers. Besides, it's time you got your *own* life. And you'd better get used to being alone, because pretty soon *I* might be gone too. Then it'll just be *you*, the *Vagina Head*, and *Vanya*. One big happy family." In one swift motion, Randy gets up and walks out the door, and as I sit there feeling like I've just been sucker punched, Franz Warner and the rest of the band follow him.

Chloe's the last to get up to leave, and when she's halfway out the door I yell, "Chloe, wait!"

She hesitates, then quickly walks over to me. "Hurry, Dylan, I want to make sure Randy's okay."

"What's he talking about? What does he mean, he might be gone soon?"

"Oh . . . Nick got a call from the manager of the Sewer Rats. They're going on tour in a month, and they asked us to be their opening band. I told the guys it's a stupid idea—that we can't just blow off school—but they're not listening to me. Anyway, right now, it's all talk, so don't worry."

"But . . . I don't understand. I mean, even if they *were* serious, it's impossible. Randy *hates* the Sewer Rats."

"I know. The whole thing's crazy, Dylan. But listen, I better go. I'll talk to you later."

I guess Doug feels sorry for me, because he brings over a whole tray of chai lattes for me and my friends and tells us they're on the house. So while my brother is out making his drug deal and formulating a plan to leave home and tour with the Sewer Rats, I hang out with Jake, Angie, and the Nerd Posse. I even manage to tolerate Jonathan talking about what a *classic* night it's turned out to be and how

Angie's film is going to have newfound depth and turmoil because of my raw honesty. The whole time, I'm feeling pretty numb, and when the Beanery is about to close I pack up my guitar, explain to everyone that I need a little time alone, then say goodbye and head home.

Inside our house it's dark and empty. As usual, I'm hungry, so I forage around in the refrigerator until I find a tray of Vanya's leftover pork and sauerkraut—which turns out to be pretty good even when it's cold—and eat until I'm stuffed. After that I head upstairs. Outside Randy's room I smell incense burning, and when I peek through the keyhole I see there's a small light on. Since Randy only burns incense when he's trying to cover up the smell of pot, I figure he scored big with Franz and is in there now getting stoned. This, along with every other sucky thing that happened tonight, really begins to infuriate me, so I push open the door and yell, "What are you gonna do now? Burn down the house?"

That's when I see Randy and Chloe in bed. Together. Thankfully they're under the covers. Randy's jeans are slung over a chair in the corner, and there's a black lace bra on the floor. Randy's box of condoms from inside his old chemistry set is sitting on his nightstand. Ribbed. Lubricated. Opened. I stand there gaping. "I . . . I'm sorry . . . I—"

"Dyl!" Randy says. "Shut the door, will you? And from now on, *knock!*"

Chloe gives me a shy smile from under the covers and waves.

I close the door and stand there for a while, breathing in

the smell of incense and listening to the bed creak. I'm not sure what to think about any of this, but I know one thing: as far as our buddy Nick is concerned, my seminude drawing of Chloe is *nothing* compared to what's going on right now in my brother's bedroom.

Thirteen

On SATURDAY I AGREE to meet up with Angie and Jonathan for another round of shooting. A big mistake, I'm sure, but after my unforgettable debut Thursday night at the Beanery, I figure I've got nothing to lose. Also, considering my questionable mental state, a day in Washington Square Park might be just what the doctor ordered. Mingling with New York's finest freaks and weirdos can only make me feel like the sanest dude on the planet.

Anyway, Saturday morning, while I'm in the kitchen pulverizing a high-energy drink complete with green tea, bee pollen, and wheat germ, Randy stumbles in. Now that he's no longer a virgin, thanks to his best friend's girlfriend, and considering a band tour with the sucky Sewer Rats, he's a little distracted. In fact, he's basically ignored me for the past couple of days. "What's up, Randy?" I say, pouring my frothy concoction into a glass. "Rough night?"

He grunts, then opens the refrigerator and pulls out a loaf of Vanya's pumpernickel bread, along with a bowl of some nasty-looking German meat pâté. Normally Vanya waits on us hand and foot, but right now she's upstairs vacuuming and singing a seriously off-key rendition of "Edelweiss." Randy takes a seat at the table and begins spreading the creamy brown mixture on a hunk of bread while I chug down my drink and watch. I know this sounds crazy, but ever since I walked in on him and Chloe the other night, I've been studying my brother closely, looking for some kind of change—an outward sign that he has indeed slept with a girl. But as far as I can tell, he's exactly the same. It's a little disappointing.

He sniffs the meat and takes a bite. "So," I say, breaking the long silence. "I hear the shredder and his metalheads are coming over today." Randy doesn't know it, but last night Headbone spilled the beans—told me that the Sewer Rats were coming to our house this afternoon to jam and discuss their upcoming tour de force with the Dead Musicians Society.

Randy stops chewing. "What's *that* supposed to mean?"

"Oh, come on, Randy. I know all about your *plans*. But honestly, I can't believe you're stooping this low. I mean, you're the one who told me that the Sewer Rats *suck* and that their lead guitarist is a shredder. Remember when we heard them play at that dive club in Canarsie? The guy's got no talent at all. He just cranks up the distortion and plays random notes on the guitar as fast as he can. He sounds like a train wreck. The rest of the band's no better."

I expect Randy to fight back, maybe even tell me where I can shove it, but he doesn't. He spreads another wad of goop on a piece of bread and takes a huge bite. "Yeah, well, I haven't heard them play in a while," he says with his mouth full. "Maybe they've changed."

"Changed?" Randy looks like he could use a drink, so I open the fridge, pour him some orange juice, and take a seat at the table. "You're just kidding yourself. Guys like that don't develop talent overnight."

He takes a long swig of the juice and plunks down the glass. "All right, fine. Whatever. Maybe they *do* suck. Maybe they have no talent at all. So what? The reason they got booked for this tour is because a lot of people like their music. If we open for them, at least we'll be playing. At least our band will get heard. Besides, you're the one who keeps telling me to play my original songs. That's what I'm planning to do. If we go on tour we can't just do covers."

What I want to tell Randy is that he's selling out, that touring with the Sewer Rats is like musical suicide for someone with his ability. But since that would probably end our discussion, I decide to focus on the more practical issues. "Well, what about wheels?" I say. "How are you going to get around? Cart all your stuff? I doubt the Sewer Rats are providing you guys with transportation."

He shrugs. "No problem. Nick's got it all worked out. Some guy he knows is hooking us up with a van. Supposedly it's a really good deal."

This sounds pretty shady to me, but I let it go and offer my next argument. "All right," I say. "What about school?

Headbone and Moser's parents will never agree to this. Dad will wig out. Mom, too, if she ever comes back."

Randy waves this away like it's nothing. "The guys aren't asking *permission* from their parents, and I don't care what Mom *or* Dad says. Besides, I only need a few more credits to graduate. I can easily make it up in the summer."

"And kiss college goodbye?"

He looks into my eyes. "Listen, Dyl, this could be our big break. Every band has to pay their dues, and if it means dropping out of school and touring with the Sewer Rats— guys who happen to have an established fan base—well, that's what we have to do. Okay? Are you finished with your interrogation?"

"Almost." My energy drink didn't exactly fill me up, so I rip off a piece of pumpernickel and sniff the pâté. "What *is* this stuff?"

"Beats me," Randy says. "But, surprisingly, it's pretty good."

I smear some on the bread and take a bite. Randy's right, it's not bad. I eat the rest of that piece and take another. Now for the most important question. "So . . . ," I say, "have you told Nick about the situation with you-know-who?"

Randy chews slowly and gives me a measured look. "Nope."

"What are you waiting for, *bro?*"

"Nothing in particular, *Dyl.*"

I'm not about to leave it there. Since I have to live vicariously through my older brother, I want details.

"Well . . . tell me. How was it?" I raise an eyebrow so Randy knows exactly what I'm talking about. S-E-X.

He keeps chewing and looks up at the ceiling, savoring his mouthful of food like it's some rare delicacy, like it's the best-tasting thing in the world. After a while, he can't help it; he grins. "It was great, dude. Awesome. Let's hope you live long enough to find out." And that's when I finally see it. The thing that's changed in Randy. He's happy. Really happy. I haven't seen him this way in a long time.

"Hey, Randy? About the other night, at the Beanery, when Franz walked in, I'm sorry, I guess I lost it, and—"

"No, you don't need to apologize, Dyl. I've been meaning to talk to you. I didn't buy any pot from Franz that night. Chloe's asked me to cut back, and I told her I would. And I'm sorry for what I said to you. I guess this thing with Mom has really gotten to me, you know? I just . . . I never thought she'd leave for good."

"Yeah," I say. "Me neither." I'm really glad to hear that Randy's planning to cut back on the weed. I just hope he can keep his promise. "Randy? If you do go on this tour, you'll come back, right?"

"Of course." He gives me a playful shove. "What do you think, you're gonna get rid of me that easily?"

As we sit there grinning at each other, Vanya pokes her head into the kitchen. "Oh, wonderful!" She walks over and places a beefy hand on each of our shoulders. "You boys found the pumpernickel and *leberwurst*. How do you like it?"

"Um, it's not bad," I say.

Randy picks up the bowl and studies the contents. "Hey, uh, Vanya? What exactly *is leberwurst*?"

"Oh, *leber* is German for *liver*. Cow's liver. *Very* nourishing for growing boys like you."

I look at Randy. "Really, did you *have* to ask?"

As planned, I meet up with Angie and Jonathan at the Ninety-fifth Street station and the three of us hop the train to Greenwich Village. The subway car is crowded, but Jonathan manages to weasel into the seat next to Angie while I take the spot across from them. As the two short-film junkies chat, pausing only to cast conspiratorial glances my way, I begin to think about what Randy said to me at the Beanery—how I should stop looking to him for answers, figure out my own life. And even though it hurts, I think about what Chloe said too. That I'm insecure, and angry about a lot of things. It's all true.

We change for the D at Thirty-sixth Street, and by the time we exit at West Fourth, I've come up with a plan. It's a new scene for the film—something that will blow Angie and Jonathan away—but more importantly, it's something for me. So while the two of them buy sodas and hot dogs from a street vendor, I cross the avenue and head for the Cage. The Cage is this totally awesome fenced-in basketball court where legends like Doctor J and Walter Berry used to play. Nowadays, the best ball handlers and shooters from all over the city—the Bronx, Brooklyn, Queens, and Manhattan—come here to jam, slam, flush, and alley-oop. I lean against the fence and watch as a game of five-on-five— shirts vs. skins—starts up. Man, I think, *if Jake knew what I was planning, he'd* freak. The two of us have always dreamed of playing inside the Cage, only that's all it's ever been: a dream. The reality would be suicide.

A few minutes later Angie and Jonathan join me, and as Angie offers me a bite of her hot dog, I look into her incredibly green eyes, and since I've already poisoned myself with mounds of Vanya's *leberwurst*, I take it. As I'm chewing and noticing the way the little blond hairs on Angie's cheek kind of glimmer in the afternoon sun, she says, "Dylan? What's wrong? You seem a little . . . I don't know, spacey."

"Oh? Do I?" I reach over and wipe a dollop of ketchup from the corner of her mouth. I consider going further—leaning in and kissing her on those full pink lips, but then I decide: first things first. So instead, I turn to Jonathan, pluck the can of soda from his hand, take a long, sugary swig, hand it back, and say, "All right, dude, listen up, time to start filming. And whatever happens, don't stop."

Angie's eyes grow wide. She peers into the court. "Dylan, you can't . . . I mean, those guys in there are like . . . *scary*."

"I've never been surer in my entire life."

There doesn't appear to be any gate leading into the Cage, so I slip in through a hole in the fence and take a seat with the guys on the sidelines who are waiting to play. Pretty soon the current game ends and a highly theatrical MC, complete with megaphone and lots of bling, struts over to us. "All right, cats! Listen to me!" He pokes his chest a few times. "I, Toulouse-Lautrec, fellow hoops enthusiast and aspiring ar*tiste*, will be calling this game. So get out there, mix it up, and find a mean-looking dude to cover." Since I happen to know that the real Toulouse-Lautrec was a Postimpressionist French painter, I'm finding this very hard to believe. But the guy *is* in charge, so I do what he says. The problem is none of the mean-looking dudes are taking me seriously, so I'm left standing there alone.

From the corner of my eye I see Toulouse-Lautrec surveying the situation. He walks over and scopes me up and down. "Listen, cat, this is the real deal. Are you serious about playing here? I mean, do you *know* where you are?"

"Um . . . yeah. It's the Cage." I glance over at Angie and Jonathan. I really don't want this guy kicking me off the court, so I say, "I want to play ball, and, well, my friend"—I point to Angie—"she's making a film. About me."

Toulouse-Lautrec peers over at Angie. Soon a big grin spreads across his face. "Well, why didn't you say so? I'm *down* with that. After all, we need to support our fellow ar*tistes* in this fine city." He raises his megaphone to his lips. "Come on now, cats! Don't leave this man hanging! Surely there's someone out there who wants to cover my friend Bony Ass!" It takes me a few seconds to realize that Toulouse-Lautrec has dubbed *me* Bony Ass. Which is really unfair, because my ass is probably the most muscular part of my body, but I'm not about to argue with the guy.

Pretty soon this short, stocky dude saunters onto the court. He points in my direction and calls out, "I'll take this sucker!" He pulls off his shirt and tosses it aside. Across his chest is a huge tattoo that reads MOTHER F.

"All *right*!" Toulouse-Lautrec shouts. "Mother Francis!

— 147 —

Coolest cat in New York City comes to save the day! Now, let's play *ball!*"

Before I know it, the game starts, and right away I find out that my only advantage against Mother F is my height. Which, in this case, really doesn't amount to much. He's stronger, quicker, and meaner, and he can trash-talk a blue streak. He really likes to show off, too, because when he gets the ball he dribbles circles around me and laughs. "Pretty dizzied up there, hey, Bony Ass? Think you're something special? Now watch this." He tries faking me out, but I call his bluff and run with him to the hole. Then, just as I'm about to block his shot, he charges into me like a freight train. I fall back, slamming my head into the fence while Mother F dunks the ball. It's pretty humiliating, but I get up and shake it off, and since Toulouse-Lautrec is busy strutting in front of the camera instead of calling the game, I decide I need a new strategy.

That's when I notice that one of the guys on my team— the one Toulouse-Lautrec calls the Grand Pupa—has got some bad blood going on with Mother F. So when Mother F gets the ball and begins taunting the Grand Pupa, calling him a variety of politically incorrect names such as *faggot, wussy boy,* and *homo,* I reach in, steal the ball, and dribble down the court for an easy layup. It happens so fast I can hardly believe it.

I guess the rest of the players are shocked too, because they just stop and stare. I glance over at Jonathan to make sure he's shooting. He is. Next to him, Angie is jumping up and down and cheering for me. *Wait till Jake sees this.*

"Let's hear it for my man Bony Ass!" Toulouse-Lautrec bellows through his megaphone.

Of course, Mother F is not pleased about this little turn of events. So the next time he gets the ball, he goes in for the kill and pulls one of the dirtiest moves in street ball—an ankle breaker, a vicious crossover that knocks me flat on my back. While I'm lying on the concrete wondering exactly how I got there, I see Jonathan running onto the court. He's calling a time-out. Angie's got the camera, and she's shooting.

I watch in disbelief as Jonathan Reed, my longtime nemesis, marches up to Mother F in an attempt to defend me. "Um, listen, brother," he says. "You need to lay off my friend Bony Ass." Jonathan, I notice, looks the way Headbone did when he stole my bottle of prescription Vicodin, popped a few, and puked his guts out in the toilet.

I figure Toulouse-Lautrec is going to intervene at this point, maybe even call a foul, but he doesn't. Instead he waves to Angie. "You go, girl! This is great stuff! Keep that camera rolling!"

Mother F seems to think this whole thing is extremely funny. He dribbles the ball, laughing at Jonathan, then tosses up a hook shot that goes in with a swish. "Oh, yeah?" he says. "And what if I *don't* lay off your friend? What if I de-cide to squash him like a little green grape? What are you going to do about it? Huh, *Romeo?*" He bats his eyelashes mockingly.

It seems pretty unfair that Jonathan gets dubbed Romeo, but since both of our lives are in danger, I'm not about to say anything. "Well, I should warn you," Jonathan says. He swallows and his Adam's apple jiggles. "I know karate. In fact"—he glances at Mother F's tattoo, takes a deep breath, and rolls up his sleeves—"I'm a mother-effin' black belt."

I'm pretty sure Jonathan is bluffing, but surprisingly, Mother F looks worried. At that moment Toulouse-Lautrec realizes he's got a job to do. He struts over and slaps the two of them on the back. "Yo, cats! Come on, enough of this! Peace, brothers! Now, let's bust it up! Shoot some hoops!"

Thankfully, Mother F agrees. So while Jonathan goes back to shooting, I get up and manage to survive the rest of the game. I don't score any more baskets, but at least I keep both feet on the ground. In the end, my team loses 7 to 5, and after Mother F does a victory dance, complete with booty shakes and power spins, he comes over to me and holds out one fist. "Hey, you did all right, Bony Ass. Sorry for giving you such a hard time."

I offer him my fist and we give each other a friendly bump. "Yeah, sure man, no problem."

"So, tell me, what's your number?" he asks.

"Number?"

"Yeah, you know, on your jersey, back home."

"Oh. Thirty-four."

"Good. I'll remember that. Wear it next time you come."

I slip out through the hole in the fence, run over, and wrap a sweaty arm around Jonathan. "Hey, thanks, dude," I say. "What you did for me out on the court—that was *tight*. I bet you don't even know karate, do you?"

Jonathan grins sheepishly and shakes his head. As the three of us leave the Cage and head toward Washington Square Park, Toulouse-Lautrec calls out, "Yo, cats! Let's hear it again for my man Bony Ass! And hey! Good luck with that movie, girl!"

Fourteen

TO CELEBRATE my fantastic feat of staying alive inside the Cage, I take Angie and Jonathan to Orgasmic Organics and order three banana–passion fruit smoothies. I suppose my opinion of Jonathan has changed somewhat, considering the fact that he stuck out his neck for me while pulling off an impressive karate bluff against Mother F, but still, I'm no idiot, so I tell the guy behind the counter to hold the ginseng on Jonathan's drink and add a double whammy to mine and Angie's. I can't control what happens in life—I guess that's up to the gods or fate or some mystical force of the universe—but I *can* decide who gets the aphrodisiacs.

Drinks in hand, we head off to Washington Square Park, and while Angie films this homeless dude sitting on a bench and feeding about a million hungry pigeons, Jonathan and I take seats on the steps around the fountain. Nearby, this really cool jazz band from New Orleans called Loose

Marbles is setting up to play. Angie and I saw them perform last summer and they were awesome.

"So, Jonathan," I say, sucking down the last of my smoothie, "what's, uh, been going on with you and Angie lately?"

He takes a sip of his impotent drink and says, "What do you mean?"

I can't believe I have to spell it out for the guy. "Come on, dude, you know what I mean. Are you two, like, in the process of getting together again? Just for the record. I'd like to know."

Jonathan sets down his cup and starts to chuckle. "Wow, Dylan, I'm surprised you even thought that was a possibility. I mean, yeah, sure, I *wish* we were together, but Angie's made it pretty clear that she just wants to be friends."

I feel this leap inside my chest, and I have to bite my bottom lip so I don't start grinning like a fool. "Ahhh, friends," I say. "Yes, I know that line quite well myself."

Jonathan, however, doesn't seem to be listening to me. He shakes his head and sighs. "The truth is, Dylan, I screwed up royally this past summer. Didn't even realize what I had until it was gone. Oh, well, hopefully what James Joyce once said is true."

I can't believe I have to put up with more of Jonathan's pretentious bullcrap. But the guy *did* sort of save my life, so I say, "Oh, yeah? And what's that?"

Dramatically, he closes his eyes and tilts his face to the sun. " 'A man's errors are his portals of discovery.' "

Of course the "error" Jonathan is referring to is his little fling with senior sex goddess Hannah Jaworski, which is pretty funny when you think about it. I mean, leave it to Jonathan Reed to turn a simple bout of teenage male horniness into a literary quest for deeper knowledge.

I give him a shove and start to laugh. His eyes pop open and he almost topples over. "Yeah, right," I say. "And I bet you had a great time on your *portal of discovery.*"

At first Jonathan seems a little offended by my blunt comment, but pretty soon he's laughing right along with me. "Well, yeah," he says. "It was nice while it lasted. But believe me, dating Hannah Jaworski, cool as it may seem, was a *huge* mistake. I learned firsthand what it means when they say 'What goes around comes around.'"

Feeling surprisingly sorry for the guy, I say, "Hey, listen, man. If it makes you feel any better, Angie was pretty messed up when you guys split. She took it real hard."

"Really?" Jonathan's face brightens. "Wow, thanks for telling me that, Dylan. Honestly, I didn't think she cared very much. At least, that's how it seemed."

I wave this away. "Eh, what do you expect? Typical Angie. In case you haven't noticed, she's got a lot of pride."

We both gaze over at Angie. She's stopped filming and is now sitting on the bench shooting the breeze with the homeless dude while a pigeon roosts on her head. Jonathan downs the last of his smoothie. "Anyway," he says, "there's really no point in me trying anymore. I don't stand a chance with you around."

I look at him. "Me? What are you talking about?"

"Oh, come on, Dylan. Even when Angie and I were

dating, all she ever did was talk about you. And if the three of us were together, it was always *you* who'd make her laugh. I never could." He sighs. "I'll probably kick myself later for admitting this, but since I'm baring my soul, I used to struggle with some pretty wicked bouts of jealousy. It was ugly."

I'm stunned by Jonathan's confession, and even more stunned that the guy envied *me*. At this point I wonder if I should bare *my* soul—confess my sadistic plans to rid the earth of Jonathan Reed—but decide that might not be a good idea. "And now Angie's making a movie about you," he goes on. "Face it, Dylan. She's obsessed."

I shake my head. "No, that's where you're wrong. Angie's obsessed with the movie. Not with me."

"*Au contraire*, my friend. I hate to burst your bubble, Dylan, but why do you think I risked my life for you out on that basketball court?" He raises an eyebrow.

"Um, I don't know, dude, why?"

"Because Angie begged me to. She was seriously freaking out. Didn't want to see her precious Dylan get hurt. Thankfully, I was able to outwit Mother F, but I'm telling you, the girl fed me to the lions!"

Aha, I think, *so now the truth comes out. Jonathan's not the valiant hero I thought he was.* But even so, I give the guy credit. He's honest. "Still, it wasn't really *me* Angie was worried about," I say. "It was the film. Think about it. If *I* got hurt she wouldn't be able to finish her movie. The reality is it's all about *Angie*. Always has been."

Jonathan purses his lips. "Well, why don't we put it to the test?" He stands up, tosses his cup in the trash, and calls out, "Hey, Angie! Come on over! Dylan and I have a new idea for the film!"

I'm not sure I like the sound of this. While Angie says goodbye to the homeless dude and makes her way to the fountain, Jonathan pulls me to my feet and explains his idea. "Listen, Dylan, all you need to do is to figure out a way to smooth Angie. Just be yourself, goof around, get her laughing. I'll capture it on tape, and when I show you the footage you'll see what I'm talking about. The girl is *totally* into you."

Angie's just a few yards away now, and suddenly a sick fear comes over me. "I don't know about this, dude," I say. "I mean, you can't just *tell* a person to be funny. It's about timing, spontaneity—"

"Exactly!" Jonathan interrupts. "Release your inhibitions and take the plunge. And remember what Kafka once said: 'My fear is my substance, and probably the best part of me.' " He gives me a shove toward Angie, takes the camera from her hands, and presses the On button. Meanwhile, Loose Marbles has begun its first number. The band features ten musicians who play New Orleans gypsy jazz on clarinet, trumpet, banjo, accordion, guitar, and washboard. The singer, a blond girl with colorful tattoos, belts out a song, while two dancers in 1940s clothing begin to swing-dance. Nearby they've cleared a spot for couples to join, and already a guy and a girl are doing a jitterbug.

I give Angie a lopsided grin. "Remember this band from last summer?"

"Sure, they're great."

Jonathan motions for me to make a move, and for lack of anything better to do I say, "Well, come on, let's go!" I take Angie's hand and pull her toward the dance circle.

"Dylan!" she protests. "What are you doing? You know I can't dance!"

This is true. Angie's a spaz. Couldn't even do the Macarena at her cousin's wedding in sixth grade. It's going to be a challenge. The guy on washboard is doing a solo now, so I start moving my feet to the beat. I've got Angie laughing, and Jonathan gives me a thumbs-up from the sidelines. Neither of us has any idea how to swing-dance, but from what I can tell, it involves twirling your partner around. A lot. So that's what I do. "It's easy," I say, giving Angie a spin. "Give it a try. Besides, look, Jonathan is filming us. You could use it in your short."

She laughs harder and twirls me around, which is not easy when you're five-four and your partner's six-three. Next is a slow, bluesy number. While the tattooed girl sings *Send me to the 'lectric chair,* I hold Angie and we slow-dance. I look into her eyes. She smiles at me. "You're really something, Dylan, you know that?"

"Yeah." Her lips are so close to mine. It's now or never. And so I do it. I kiss her. The most amazing thing is that Angie kisses me back. I even hear a small, pleasurable moan escape from her throat. The double whammy of ginseng is really kicking in, and I don't want to stop. But the next thing I know, Angie's hands are on my chest. She pushes me away and walks out of the circle. I follow her. "Angie, wait!"

She marches up to Jonathan. "You guys . . . you planned

this whole thing, didn't you? What was it, some kind of a dare?"

Jonathan shrugs guiltily. "Um, not really. More of a . . . an experiment, I guess."

I glare at him. The dude's honesty is really starting to annoy me.

"Experiment?" Angie says. "Well, isn't that nice? All right, I can tell you guys right now, that scene is *not* going to be in my film. In case you don't realize, the whole beauty of this project is that nothing is staged or forced. The action is natural. I thought the two of you understood that."

What I want to say to Angie is that kissing her seemed totally natural to me, but instead I hold out my hands and say, "Sorry, Angie. I didn't mean to mess up your film."

For a moment it looks like she's about to say something. Instead, she grabs her camera from Jonathan and storms off.

"See, Dylan, what did I tell you?" Jonathan says. "The girl is *obsessed*."

While Angie cools down by the dog run and Jonathan tries his luck against one of the chess hustlers, I stroll to the other side of the park, take a seat on a bench near the hangman's elm, and try to figure out what just happened between Angie and me. After a few minutes, I decide that I'm still clueless when it comes to girls, so instead I focus my attention on this young, classy-looking black dude on the opposite side of the path. He's playing an alto sax. At first I'm struck by his appearance—he's tall, way taller than me, with broad shoulders, huge hands, and a headful of long, thick, silky cornrows. But after listening to him for a while I realize that the guy is a really good musician. In fact, he's excellent.

After he performs an old blues tune that I vaguely recognize, he starts to play "Little Wing" by Jimi Hendrix. It makes me smile because it's one of the songs Randy does really well on guitar. As I sit there listening to the deep moan of the sax, in my mind I fill in all the spaces with Randy's intricate riffs. Soon I forget all the sucky things that have happened to me lately, including Angie's latest stunt of pushing me away when I was so into kissing her.

When the song is over, I reach into my pocket and pull out a few singles, but as I walk across the path I realize that the guy doesn't have his case open. He's sitting down now, cleaning the mouthpiece of his sax with a cloth. I hold out the bills. "Dude," I say, "that was awesome. Here."

He glances at the cash and waves it away. "Oh, no, you got it wrong, man. I don't play for money." He goes back to cleaning.

"Oh, sorry," I say, stuffing the bills back into my pocket. "I just . . . well, I really enjoyed hearing you play."

He looks up and smiles. "Yeah, I know. I saw you over there, dreaming away on that bench. Are you a Hendrix fan?"

There is something so cool about this guy, I almost want to ask if I can shake his hand in the hopes that some of it will rub off on me. "Sure," I say, "I like Hendrix, but my brother, Randy—he's a huge fan. He plays lead guitar and performs a lot of Hendrix's music."

He nods, studying me. "How about you? You play?"

"Um, yeah, I do. Mostly classical guitar now, but I used to play a good amount of rock and blues."

"Well." He shrugs. "I've got time for one more song. Want to join me?" To my surprise, he reaches behind the bench, pulls out a guitar case, and sets it on the ground. "A friend of mine was supposed to show, but he never did. It's a nice piece. Looks like your name is written all over it."

I stare at the case in front of me. My stomach is filling with butterflies, and there's a very good chance that I'll screw up and make a fool of myself, but when I look into the dude's eyes I realize that none of that matters. "Yeah, sure," I say. "Why not?"

After I warm up for a few minutes, we toss around a few ideas and decide on an old Buddy Guy song called "First Time I Met the Blues." Mostly I strum while the sax takes the lead, and even though I'm a little rusty, I do all right. While we play, I look around for Angie and Jonathan, thinking this would be a pretty cool thing to capture on camera, but I don't see them anywhere. We wind up jamming for a long time, and when the song finally ends we shake hands and introduce ourselves. I find out that the guy's name is Paul; he's a music major at NYU.

"Listen, Dylan," he says as we're packing up the instruments. "Next Saturday my friends and I are having a jam session at the student lounge at Sixth and Waverly. Why don't you come? Invite your brother, too. It's a real good time. We start about seven-thirty, end about two." He snaps the last buckle on his saxophone case. I hand him the guitar.

"All right," I say. "Maybe I will."

As he takes off down the path, I watch, committing what he said to memory. Next Saturday. Student lounge. Sixth and Waverly. Seven-thirty. Randy is invited. A minute later Paul disappears through the triumphal arch.

As I stand there in the middle of the park, I suddenly realize that there is a place in Greenwich Village I need to visit before I return home today. A place I should have gone a long time ago. It's at First and Lafayette. Philippe LeBlanc's studio.

"Dylan?" I turn around and see Angie. She's standing several feet away, and she looks upset.

"Hey." I walk over and gently take her hand. "What's going on?"

She hangs her head. "Listen, about before . . . I'm sorry. I didn't mean to say what I did. It's just, well, everything happened so fast, and honestly, Dylan, I'm not ready for—"

"Whoa, whoa, Angie, it's all right. Everything's cool. I understand."

"You do?" She looks up.

"Yeah, sure. And right now, I need to ask you, my best friend, for a favor. There's a place I have to go, and I'd like if you'd come with me."

Fifteen

ANGIE AND I GRAB JONATHAN, who's already lost twenty bucks to the chess hustlers, and the three of us head south toward First and Lafayette. Along the way I think back to the last time I spoke with my mother. It was a few days before my arrest; she was getting ready for her trip to Paris and had called and asked if Randy and I would stop by Philippe's studio. She wanted to say goodbye and to show us some of her pieces on display.

"You can't be serious, Mom," I said. "I mean, you're the one who walked out on us. And now you're off to Paris, and you want us to *stop by* Philippe's studio? Just like that? I don't think so."

There was silence on the other end, and after a while a sniffle. She was crying. *Good*, I thought. *Let her cry.* "Dylan? Honey, listen, I know this is hard for you. It is for me, too, but please, try to understand—"

I didn't let her say one more word. I slammed down the phone and walked away. She didn't call back.

Now, as we reach First and Lafayette, I stop outside Philippe's place and peer through the window. It's a combination studio–art gallery where Philippe works and sells his paintings along with pieces by some other artists in the neighborhood. Inside, customers are milling about and the receptionist is answering questions. I don't see what I'm looking for, so I continue through a winding passage that leads to a back room filled with more paintings. Angie and Jonathan follow. When I see my mother's pieces hanging on the wall, I almost fall over.

There are three, and I recognize each image from old family photographs. The first is a watercolor of Randy when he was six or seven. He's sitting atop my dad's car and plucking this old, beat-up ukulele with a look of pure determination on his face. The next is a pastel of me strolling through our little garden in the backyard when I was two or three. In one of my hands is a rusty watering can, and in the other a huge yellow rose.

But the one that really gets to me is the third piece. It's an oil painting of my dad standing outside Jerry's Ice Cream Parlor in Brooklyn. Randy, a toddler, is pressed up against his leg, slurping down what looks like a root beer float, and I, a baby, am seated on my dad's hip with my mouth open, ready to take a bite of his cone. The way my mother painted it, you can't tell where one of us begins and the other ends.

"Excuse me, miss? Please, put away the camera. You're

not allowed to take pictures inside the gallery." I turn around and see Angie filming my mother's paintings. She's in kind of a trance and doesn't seem to hear the receptionist. "Miss, I said put away the camera."

I look at Jonathan; he shrugs. Next I hear a familiar voice saying, "No, no, Sarah, it's all right. I know them." There are footsteps across the wood floor. I turn and face Philippe. "Dylan? I . . . thought that was you."

It's kind of funny. I spent the past few months trying to hate the dude, but suddenly I remember how much I used to like him. Unlike Jonathan Reed, Philippe is the kind of person who could get away with being pretentious if he wanted to, since he's this really great artist and a renowned professor and owns this fabulous studio to boot, but the truth is he's pretty humble and a genuinely nice guy. I look around the room. It's no wonder my mother left us for him. For this new life in the Village. Given the choice, who wouldn't? "Yeah, well, I was in the neighborhood," I say, "so I figured I'd stop by."

He nods. "I'm glad you did. Your mother was so eager for you to see these pieces before we left. We would have taken them to Paris, but the show was strictly abstract. Anyway, she'll be right back. She just stepped out for coffee. We're both a little jet-lagged." He motions toward the wall. "But tell me, what do you think?"

I look at the paintings and a hot lump wells up in my throat. They're good—great, even—but I can't help feeling betrayed. Why should my mother be allowed to paint *us*? Hang our family's memories on the wall of Philippe's studio for the whole world to see? It doesn't seem fair. "Um, I don't know, I—"

Suddenly I feel a hand on my back. It's Angie. "Dylan," she whispers. "Your mom's here. Why don't you talk to her? Jonathan and I will wait for you outside."

I turn and see my mom standing in the hallway. She's holding a tray with two foam cups. She's dressed in clothes I've never seen before—a multicolored scarf, an alpaca sweater, suede boots with long fringes. No more doctor's wife. Now it's my mother, the hippie. She looks happy to see me and frightened at the same time. Angie and Jonathan disappear down the hallway. Philippe goes over and takes the tray from my mom's hand. Before he leaves, he gives her shoulder a gentle squeeze. Suddenly, we're alone.

"Dylan?" she says, taking a few steps toward me. Already I can smell her. Milled soap with lavender. When I was a kid and I had a fever she'd put a cool washcloth on my forehead that smelled of the same thing. Part of me wants to run over and hug her the way I did when I was little, when she and my dad would return from a long trip, but my feet are pinned to the floor. "I'm so glad you came, honey. I called the house earlier, but—"

"Why'd you do it?" I demand, pointing to the wall. "Why'd you paint *us*? You had no right."

She stops and opens her mouth, but nothing comes out.

"What do you think, Mom? You can paint a few pictures and pretend like everything's okay? Like we're one big happy family?"

"No," she says, in barely a whisper. "That's not what I—"

"Face it, Mom. You left. You just picked up and *left*. And now, do you even know what's going on at home? Do you have *any* clue?"

"I . . . think I might, but—"

"Well, just in case you don't, let me fill you in. You see, Dad doesn't really live with us anymore. He camps out at the hospital. But whenever he does show up, he sits for hours in your studio, petting your mangy three-legged cat and staring into space like a zombie. And then there's Randy, who gets stoned all the time with his idiotic friends. He doesn't draw anymore, doesn't even write his own music. And then of course there's me, the one who's left holding it all together." I can feel the blood pounding in my ears. It's the most I've said to my mother in months, and it feels good.

"Dylan," she says, taking a few more steps toward me. "I understand that you're angry, and you have a right to be. I'm concerned about your father and Randy and you. But sometimes life isn't so simple. People have to make their own decisions. We need to talk, work things out. All of us. I'm planning to come home next weekend. Maybe we can sit down and—"

"Forget it," I say. "Don't bother. Just . . ." I point to the wall. "Talk to your paintings. I'm sure they'll tell you everything you want to hear." I walk past her. "Hope you had a *great* time in Paris." I race through the winding hall and out the front door. I hear my mother calling my name, but I don't turn around.

As promised, Angie and Jonathan are waiting for me

outside. "Let's go," I say. "I never want to come back here again."

Angie doesn't ask any questions. She just holds my hand on the train ride back to Brooklyn. The three of us get off at Ninety-fifth Street and walk silently along the water. "Call me, Dylan," Angie says when we reach her house. "I'll be working on edits tonight, but you're welcome to come over."

"Thanks," I say. "But I don't think I'd be much company." I kiss her on the cheek and give Jonathan one of those lame slap-grip handshakes. "Later, dude," I say. "Thanks for saving my butt inside the Cage."

He nods. "Again, Dylan, the saying holds true. 'A man's errors are his portals of discovery.' "

When I get home I'm greeted by a cacophony of drums, guitars, and heavy-metal screeches thumping through the floorboards of our house. The Sewer Rats are in the basement, and their music is a perfect backdrop for the battle raging inside our kitchen. My dad, still in his scrubs, is pacing the floor and ranting about ungrateful teenagers and their asinine ideas while Randy leans against the refrigerator, arms across his chest. Vanya is waving around a teakettle, yelling, "Dr. Fontaine! Randy! Please, sit down! I'll make tea!"

When my dad sees me, his eyes grow wild. "Dylan! Tell me right now. Did you know about this?" I don't think I've ever seen him this delirious. He points accusingly at Randy.

"Did you know your brother was planning to drop out of school and go on tour with those . . . those *freaks* in our basement?"

Uh-oh. Now the shit has really hit the fan. "Um . . ." I look at Randy, wondering who spilled the beans. Maybe Moser, but probably Headbone in a Heineken-induced stupor. Randy's eyes meet mine for a second; then he does this fake yawn that really pisses off my dad. I'd like to tell my father that I think Randy is making a huge mistake, but right now I don't think that will fly. "Well," I say. "Yeah, I sort of knew. I guess."

My dad throws up his hands. "You *sort of* knew? I don't believe this!" He goes back to pacing the floor. "Well, that's just great. I guess I'm the last one to find out. And now I have to tell your mother." He stops and glares at Randy. "I must say, Randy, you picked the perfect day to drop the bomb. The day she returns from Paris. Right when she was looking forward to seeing you."

Randy snorts and mumbles something under his breath. This *really* sets my dad off. "What was that?" he demands. "What did you just say?"

My stomach tightens. *No, Randy, don't.*

Defiantly, he looks at my dad. "I said, 'Yeah, right.' As if Mom really cares. Like she really wants to see us. You know, for once, I wish someone in our screwed-up family would just come out and say the truth. That Mom left us for some hotshot artist in the Village so she could pursue her *career*, whatever that means. And that *you*, Dad, hate being around your own kids, so you hire a maid to cook and

— 168 —

clean and make sure the police don't show up at our front door."

"Watch your mouth, Randy!" my dad says.

"Oh, no," Randy goes on. "I'm finished with that. I don't have to listen to you. Remember? I'm leaving. And now"— he gestures toward me—"you'll have *one* perfect son. The kid who does everything right. The one who *never* screws up. You think I'm stupid, Dad? You think I don't know how much you'd *love* to get rid of me?"

My dad is so angry, he's shaking. An animal noise rises in his throat. He bolts toward Randy and smacks him across the face. "Get out!" he screams. "Get out of here, now!"

Vanya gasps in horror.

"Dad!" I say, pulling him away. "Stop! Don't!"

It takes Randy a moment to register what's happened. My father has never hit either one of us before. Randy touches the side of his face and blinks a few times. The room is quiet; all you can hear is the water beginning to simmer in the teakettle. In the basement the music has stopped, and the next thing I hear are feet pounding up the stairs. The door swings open and out walk Moser, Headbone, and Nick, followed by four members of the Sewer Rats decked out in black leather, chains, and thick eyeliner. "Get out, all of you!" my dad yells. "You're not welcome here!" Quickly they file out the back door.

Randy glares at my father. Randy's fists are clenched. It looks like he might strike back, but he doesn't. He grabs his jacket and bolts. The door slams behind him.

My first instinct is to run after Randy, but I don't because I know he'll just curse me out and tell me to go home. I look around the room. I feel lost. Vanya pulls out a chair. "Come, Dylan," she says pleadingly. "Sit down. Talk to your father. We'll have tea and I'll warm some strudel."

I shake my head. "No, Vanya. It's too late for that." I look at my dad. There are tears in his eyes, but I don't feel any pity for him. Not now. Not after what he just did. "Randy's right, Dad," I say. "You *don't* care. You never have. And when Mom left us, you did nothing to stop her. *Nothing*. You just let her go. This whole thing's *your* fault. And now, in just a few weeks, Randy will be gone, and who knows what'll happen to him out there? And guess what, Dad? He's the only person I have left!"

"Dylan, wait, let's talk!" Dad calls. But it's too late. A second later I'm out the front door.

I run to the water and walk along the path—all the way to the Sixty-ninth Street pier. It's getting dark now, but I can still make out the Statue of Liberty, a tiny green speck in the distance. The wind is blowing and I'm cold and tired and sick of being alone with no one to talk to, so I turn around. I stop by Angie's house on the way home, but when I get there I glance up at her bedroom window and see her sitting at the computer with Jonathan, editing the film. They're laughing and looking like they're having a blast, so instead of knocking on her door I head over to Jake's. I feel this urgent need now to tell Jake about my game inside the Cage—about Mother F and the Grand Pupa and Toulouse-Lautrec and how I actually scored a basket. But when I reach his house, it's dark and empty. No one's there.

There's nothing left to do but go home. Inside our house it's dark except for a light on in my mom's studio. My dad's in there, I'm sure, sitting by my mom's half-finished portrait, petting Tripod. Dad's like a monk keeping vigil before some holy shrine. I lock my door and climb into bed, hoping he'll leave me alone. But a few minutes later he knocks. "Dylan? May I come in?"

"No. Go away."

"Please, Dylan. I'm sorry. I shouldn't have hit your brother. It was wrong. I was angry, and . . . well, there's no excuse. I just wanted to tell you that I feel terrible about it. When Randy comes home I'll apologize. We'll work things out. I promise." He stands there awhile longer, hoping, I guess, that I'll give in, tell him it's okay, but I don't. Soon he shuffles across the hallway. I hear the click of his bedroom door.

There's a gnawing in my stomach and it dawns on me that I should have eaten dinner, but now the whole day crashes in on me and I'm so tired I can barely move. I curl up into a ball and drift off to sleep. I dream that I'm in Philippe's studio again, walking through the narrow, winding passage, only this time it goes on and on; I'm like a rat in a maze and I can't find the back room and my mother's paintings.

* * *

In the middle of the night someone climbs into my bed. A hairy leg bumps against mine. "Hey, Dyl, I picked your lock. Is it all right if I sleep here?"

It's Randy. I glance at the clock. Three a.m. "Um, yeah, sure." I'm pretty groggy, but I can tell Randy wants to talk. It's this game we used to play when we were young. In the middle of the night, if one of us was scared or lonely or had a bad dream, we'd climb into the other one's bed, pretend nothing was wrong, and start shooting the breeze. "What's up, dude?" I say.

Randy is lying on his back, hands tucked behind his head. "Nick was in Mom's studio this afternoon. He saw your drawing of Chloe hanging on the wall."

"Oh?" I sit up a little. "So . . . what's the deal? Am I a dead man?"

"No," Randy says. "Lucky for you, Nick didn't notice your initials at the bottom, so he thought I drew it. I let him believe I did. Later I told him the truth about me and Chloe. I figured no more secrets. Not if we're going on tour together."

"Uh-oh," I say. "Thanks for saving my hide, but now it looks like *you're* the dead man. What happened?"

"Oh, he was pissed. We got into a pretty bad argument—he even threw a punch—but I'm hoping it'll all blow over in the morning."

This sounds like wishful thinking to me, but I don't tell Randy that. "Are you all right?"

"Yeah, I guess. I had to do it, though, you know?"

"I know." We lie there for a while, and I'm glad my

brother is right next to me. It's been a long time, almost a year, since we talked, *really* talked, or spent time together. I haven't thought about it lately, but suddenly I realize how much I've missed him. "I stopped by Philippe's studio today," I say. "I saw Mom."

He turns to me. "Really? How'd that go?"

"Um, pretty bad, actually. It was weird—she painted these pictures of you and me—even Dad—from old photographs. They're hanging in the gallery. When I saw them, I . . . sort of flipped out."

"Yeah, well, I can understand why. I mean, paintings of *us*? That's messed up." He shakes his head. "Glad I wasn't there."

Neither of us says anything for a while, and before long I'm thinking about Angie. Now that my brother has a girlfriend, I wonder if he has any words of wisdom to share. "Randy? When you and Chloe got together, how did it happen? How did you know it was the right time to tell her how you feel?"

He turns and studies me. I'm glad the room is dark. "I don't know, Dyl, I guess I got sick of being a chicken—afraid to take a chance—so I just went for it. I figured, whatever happened, at least I tried."

I wonder what happens when you take a chance and it backfires. "Yeah, I see what you mean," I say. "Anyway, I'm glad it worked out for you and Chloe."

"Me too. So how's Angie's film going? Any more shoots?"

"Yep. We did a few in the Village today. I scored a basket inside the Cage."

"What? No way! You kidding me?"

"Nope. Almost got killed, but I did it. Oh, and afterward I met this really cool guy at Washington Square Park—a sax player named Paul. He played 'Little Wing' and I tried to give him a couple of bucks, but he wouldn't take it. Anyway, he had this guitar and we played a blues piece together and then he invited *us* to come to a jam session next Saturday at NYU. I told him about you, how you liked Hendrix and played a lot of his music. I'm telling you, Randy, the two of you would sound *sweet* together."

Randy doesn't say anything for a long time. Finally, he turns to me. "Did you say next Saturday?"

"Yeah. Seven-thirty at the student lounge at Sixth and Waverly. Will you come?"

He nods. "All right. Maybe I will."

Suddenly I don't feel so bad. Like maybe things will work out after all. And now I have something to look forward to. Randy and I playing together. Like old times.

"Hey, Dyl?" Randy says. "Listen, I'm sorry about this afternoon when I was going off on Dad, telling him how he'd be left with one perfect son. I shouldn't have dragged you into it."

"It's all right. I just . . . I felt really bad when Dad hit you. He's sorry. He told me so. I'm sure he'll apologize tomorrow."

"Eh, don't worry about it," Randy says. "Besides, I was being a punk. Probably deserved it."

Soon I hear Randy's breathing become slow and steady. I nudge him a little. "Hey, Randy? Listen, you're not going to bag on me, right? You'll come to that jam session next Saturday?"

He holds up a hand in the dark and I grip it, tight. "Listen, bro," he says. "As long as Nick doesn't kill me first, I'll be there. You got my word."

Sixteen

NICK DOESN'T KILL RANDY, but according to the Dead Musicians Society's code of honor, he commits the next-worst crime: he disappears. Skips band practice Sunday afternoon and doesn't show up for school Monday morning. No one knows where he is. To pass the time, Randy asks me to fill in on rhythm guitar so the band can at least run through its songs until Nick cools off, but by Tuesday everyone is getting pretty antsy. "Moser!" Headbone shouts as we finish up Nirvana's "Smells Like Teen Spirit." "Dude, that seriously *sucked*. I'm telling you, man, Kurt's rolling over in his grave right now!"

Moser, who's been subbing for Nick on vocals, sets down his bass and flops onto the sofa. He throws up his hands in despair. "I'm sorry, guys. I know Kurt deserves better. But what can I say? It's impossible to come close to the man's genius. Honestly, I don't know how Nick does it."

The rest of us glare at Headbone until he sighs, hops off his drum stool, and puts an arm around Moser. "Hey, it's all right, *compadre*. I know it's tough, but you're doing just fine. Really. Besides, none of this is your fault."

Moser nods. "Yeah, you got that right. I mean, I'm not the one who . . ." He stops midsentence. Everyone is quiet.

"Uh-oh," Headbone says. "Trouble."

Randy sets down his guitar. "You're not the one who *what*, Moser?"

"Well . . ." Moser glances around the room. "If you want the truth, Randy, I'm not the one who screwed everything up. I mean, what happened to the Dead Musicians Society's code of honor? I thought chicks weren't supposed to come between us."

I expect Chloe to protest, fling a shoe at Moser, tell him he'd better not use derogatory terms for women in her presence ever again. But she doesn't. She just stands there looking lost. It scares me.

"Yeah," Headbone chimes in. "Moser's right. What happened to *that*?"

Soon a tear slides down Chloe's cheek. When Randy sees it he rushes over and wraps his arms around her. She hangs her head. "They're right," she says. "It's all my fault."

"No," Randy says. He whispers something in her ear, but she's inconsolable.

Meanwhile, I stand up and give Headbone and Moser my iciest stare. I seriously want to wrap the neck of my guitar around the two imbeciles' necks. "Why don't you guys just *shut up* for once?" I say. "Can't you see Chloe's upset?

Besides, maybe you should lay off Randy and ask *Nick* a few questions about loyalty, about codes of honor. Look around, guys. In case you haven't noticed, *he's* the one who went AWOL."

The room grows quiet again. Finally, Chloe steps away from Randy. "I'm going to Nick's house," she says. "Talk some sense into him."

Randy shakes his head. "No, Chloe. Please. Don't." He sounds desperate. "I mean . . . how do you even know Nick's home?"

She hesitates for a moment. "He is. He called me this morning. Said he wants to talk things over. At first I said no, there was nothing to discuss, but now I think I'd better go. For the sake of the band."

Randy blinks a few times. "Wait. I'll come with you. We'll both talk to him. No matter what, Nick is my best friend. He'll listen to me."

"No, Randy," Chloe says emphatically. "This is something I have to do alone. Privately. It's between me and Nick."

Randy reaches out to her, but she takes another step back and heads for the stairs. Headbone and Moser send each other eyebrow messages. "I won't be long," Chloe says. "I'll call if there's a problem. Just . . . keep practicing. And don't worry, everything will work out."

"Chloe, wait!" Randy follows her up the stairs, and you can hear him asking for a kiss goodbye. Moser, Headbone, and I feign lack of interest, but we're all dying to know what's going on up there.

When Randy returns, Headbone reaches into his pocket and pulls out an old Altoids box filled with joints. "Randy, dude," he says. "Listen, it's Tuesday, right? And you know what that means." He grins. "Attila the Hun's day off. Come on, man, enough practicing. Let's get *lit*."

Moser looks at the box of joints; he's practically salivating. "Awesome idea, Headbone." He plucks one out and closes his eyes. "Maybe now I can dull the pain of botching Kurt's masterpiece."

I give Moser a hard shove and he falls onto the sofa. "Yeah, right," I say. "Break out the violins, will you?"

"Hey, come on, Dyl," Moser says. "I'm in serious agony!" He points to his neck. "And look, my eczema is flaring up again."

Headbone takes out a joint and offers it to Randy. "Here, man, it'll help pass the time, anyway. Keep your mind off . . . you know, things."

I watch, wondering what Randy's going to do. It's not like he's been a saint since he pledged to Chloe to cut back on the weed, but as far as I can tell he's been trying. "Nah, that's all right," he says. "You guys go ahead. Honestly, the last thing I want right now is to be high."

Moser eagerly digs into his pocket for a book of matches, but before he can light up, Headbone snatches the joint from his hand. "No way, Moser!" he says. "If Randy's not smoking, then neither are we. We're the Dead Musicians Society and we stick together."

Moser stands there with his mouth hanging open. I must say, Headbone's pledge of sobriety is rather commendable. I pat him on the back and sit next to Randy. "We're here for you, bro. No matter what."

Time passes, and all you can hear is the clock ticking and the refrigerator humming. Before long Moser and Headbone fall asleep on the sofa, but I keep watch with Randy. Neither of us says much, and after a while I put on an old Grateful Dead tape that I bought at a garage sale last year. The music is mellow and soothing. I'm hoping it will relax Randy. In the middle of "Uncle John's Band" the phone rings. We both jump. "I'll get it," I say. "I'll let you know if it's her."

I run upstairs and pick up on the fourth ring. "Dylan, is that you?" Chloe says. Her voice is hushed and panicky.

"Yeah, it's me. Hold on a sec, I'll get Randy—"

"No!" she says. "There's no time. Listen carefully. The police were just here. Nick's in a lot of trouble. I'm not sure, but I think they have Randy's name and address too. They might be driving to your place right now. They have dogs, Dylan, so you have to be quick. Remember that spot in the backyard where Randy showed us his stash?"

My heart is pounding. My knees begin to buckle. "Um, yeah."

"Dig it up. There's half a kilo there now. Get rid of it. Hurry!"

Without even thinking I slam down the phone and run downstairs. "Randy!" I shake Moser and Headbone and quickly tell them the news. They stare at me in disbelief. "Come on!" As we race upstairs I start giving orders. "Moser, you keep watch out front. If the police show up, stall them.

Headbone, keep a lookout for Mr. Pellegrino or any other suspicious neighbors. Randy, you and me will dig it up. Let's go!"

Moser and Headbone take their positions while Randy and I race to the backyard. We find the spot and sift through leaves and loose dirt. I pull out the box. Beneath it the metric scale from McKinley High glints in the sun. I glare at Randy. "So I'm imagining things, huh, bro?" I open the box. Inside is a huge bag of purple-bud, just like the one under the floorboards in my mom's studio. "You're such a liar!" I say. "You've been dealing all along!" I throw the bag at him. "I hope you get arrested—you and your stupid friends!"

But when I look at Randy's face I suddenly realize that he's seeing this bag of weed for the first time. It's lying beside his dirty knees. He won't even touch it. "Dylan, I swear to God, I don't know how that got here. I've never seen it before."

And then it all comes to me. "Nick!" I say. "*He's* the one dealing. Hiding his weed on our property so he won't get busted. Dude, he probably gave your name to the police, too. Sold you out over a girl! Wow, that's some friend you got, Randy."

At that moment Moser's head pokes around the side of the house. "Dudes, your dad's here! He just turned the corner! Let's bail!"

"Hurry!" Headbone yells. He tosses his Altoids box, and it lands in a backyard past Mr. Pellegrino's house. "The coast is clear! Run!"

I grab the bag of weed and stuff it up my shirt. "Get rid of the scale, Randy. I'll take care of this. Is there anything else in the house?"

"No, nothing." His face is pale. A cold wind is blowing, but beads of sweat line his upper lip. "Dylan, listen, you don't have to stick your neck out for me, man, I mean—"

"Look. Just tell Dad I'm at the park shooting hoops or something. I'll catch up with you later."

I take a quick glance at old man Pellegrino's window. It's dark inside his house, and the curtains are drawn. I quickly hop his fence. I race toward the water, and when I reach Shore Road I see two police cars turn up our street. I hit the path and keep running until I'm completely out of breath. There's an iron railing bordering this section of the bay, and on the other side are jagged black rocks leading to the water. I look around and wait for two kids on bikes to pass. Then I jump the railing. Once my feet are firmly planted on the rocks below, I reach inside my shirt, break open the plastic bag, and dump its contents into the bay. The sweet-smelling purplish-brown buds float lazily along the waves. For a moment I wonder if the fish will nibble at them. I imagine a crab saying to his friend, "Hey, dude, try this stuff! It'll blow your mind!" I wait for two joggers to pass, and then I hop the fence back onto the path. As far as I can tell, not a soul has seen what I've just done.

After my crime, I go to the only place I want to be right now. Angie's. I hope she's home. And even though I've come to the conclusion that Jonathan Reed is not the pretentious jackass I originally thought he was, I hope to God Angie's alone. There are some things you can only share with your best friend. A minute later she answers the door. She's wearing a fuzzy blue bathrobe and her hair is wrapped up in a towel. Cotton balls are stuffed between her toes, and on her toenails is shiny red polish. I've lucked out. "Dylan? Oh, my God, are you okay?"

It's only then that I realize I'm shivering. The sun has set behind the houses now and there's a fierce wind kicking up. I'm wearing only jeans and a threadbare T-shirt. Angie pulls me inside, and after she's made me drink a cup of steaming hot tea, we go to her room and I tell her everything. I tell her about the weed under the floorboards and hidden underground in our backyard, how Nick's been dealing and hiding his dope on our property, and how he ratted on Randy, all because of Chloe. I tell her how I just dumped half a kilo of purple-bud into the bay off Shore Road and started daydreaming about fish and crabs getting high. "So, technically," I say, "I'm an accomplice to a crime."

Angie nods. "Technically, yes. But theoretically, Dylan, you're more of a hero."

"Yeah, right," I say. "Tell that to the police." I sit up and start plucking the cotton balls from between Angie's toes. I toss them, one by one, into the little tin trash can sitting in the far corner of the room. "I'm afraid to go home, Angie. I'm afraid the police have already arrested Randy and are waiting for me."

"I'll come with you," she says. She sits up and pulls the towel off her head. Her long, coppery hair hangs loose and damp over her robe. "It'll be all right, Dylan. Your father will know what to do. And if Randy's in trouble, it'll be his first offense. They'll go easy on him. That's the way it works. And . . . no one saw *you*, right?"

I shrug. "Yeah. As far as I know."

"Good. I'll dry my hair and get dressed and the two of us will go over there together."

About ten minutes later, Angie and I set out for my house. As I suspected, two police cars are parked outside, and when I open the front door I see my father speaking to an officer. Beside the cop sits a German shepherd, panting quietly. When the dog sees me his ears perk up. My heart stops. "Dylan!" my dad says. "Thank God you're home. Hi, Angie." Angie nods a quick hello. "This is important, Dylan. Do you know where Randy is?"

"No," I say, eyeing the dog. Angie takes my hand and gives it a squeeze. On the way over we talked about how I have to remain calm, feign ignorance, and lie if necessary. But it doesn't come naturally. "Why, Dad? What's . . . going on?"

My dad glances at the officer, who seems truly sorry to be bothering a nice, well-mannered obstetrician and his poster-boy-for-a-better-America son in their own home. Jeez, if he only knew. "Dylan," my dad says, his face pale and drawn. "This is Officer Redgrave. Apparently someone gave Randy's name to the police. Said he was dealing marijuana."

"Oh, that's weird." I wonder if I sound convincing. Probably not. "Um, who was it?"

"I don't know. Unfortunately, the police can't give us that information. Anyway, Randy wasn't here when I got home. The officers just finished their search. They found nothing, but they need to talk to him. Follow up on some possible leads. Apparently Nick's house has already been searched. I've called the rest of Randy's friends, but no one seems to be around. Do you have any idea where he is?"

Suddenly, the dog gets up and starts sniffing my hands. He sticks his wet nose up my shirt. Beads of sweat break out on my forehead. For lack of a better idea, I kneel down and scratch the suspicious mutt behind his ears. I glance at the officer, but he doesn't seem to notice anything unusual. Just a friendly kid petting a dog. "No, Dad," I say. "I have no clue."

"All right, then." He offers the cop his hand. They shake. "Officer Redgrave, I'll let you know when my son returns."

"Yes, thank you, Dr. Fontaine. I'm sorry for the trouble."

"No trouble at all," my dad says. "I understand. And good luck with your investigation."

Randy doesn't return home that night, and he doesn't show up the following morning. Frantically, my dad and I call his friends, teachers, acquaintances, anyone who may have seen him in the past twenty-four hours. No one knows where he is. I find out from Headbone that Nick is on house arrest. Apparently the police found some weed in his room, but not enough to press charges for distribution. The snake in the grass has tempted fate and won. For now. In a fit of rage, I hop onto my bike and ride to his place. "Where is he?" I demand. "Where's my brother?"

"I don't know, Dylan, I swear."

We're in Nick's bedroom. The door is closed and his parents are downstairs. I point to the metal bracelet on his ankle. "There's no, like, microphone on that thing, is there?"

"No," he says. "It's just a tracker. If I leave the house, the cops find out."

"All right, then." I march up to Nick and look him straight in the eye. "I know what you've been doing all along, dude. Stashing weed in our house, in our backyard. We *all* know. Your game's up. And now you gave the police Randy's name, didn't you? Hung your best friend out to dry. Just to get back at him for hooking up with Chloe. The girl he's crazy about."

"No," he says. "You got it wrong, Dylan. Yeah, I hid the weed in your house, and in your backyard, but it was only temporary until I could move it somewhere else. It was never there for more than a day or two. You see, the band needed money for the tour, for the van—that's the only reason I did it. I knew Randy wouldn't agree, none of the guys would, so I kept it a secret. And sure, I was pissed about him and Chloe, but you got to believe me, Dylan, I'd never rat him out. It was *Franz*. He's the one. He got busted, and the cops told him he'd have less jail time if he gave them some names. Next thing I knew, they were knocking on my door."

It feels like someone has just punched me in the stomach. I think about what I said to Randy. How I blamed Nick for giving his name to the police. Deep down, I know that's why Randy ran. Why he hasn't come home. He thought Nick betrayed him in the worst possible way. "You had no right," I say. "You had no right to put Randy in danger. To put all of us in danger."

"I know that, Dylan. And I'm sorry. I swear, I'd do anything to take it back. I never thought it would turn out this way. Listen, I can't leave the house, but I'll make some calls. I'll find out where Randy is. I promise. When I hear something I'll let you know."

I look at Nick. Surprisingly, there are tears in his eyes. He looks scared, but not for himself. For Randy. I muster everything inside me to hate his guts, but I can't. Right now I can only hate myself.

That evening, my dad calls my mother. After hearing the news, she's at our doorstep in less than an hour. The three of us go to the police station and file a missing persons report. When the detective interviews my parents and discovers all the problems we've been having at home, he checks off the box labeled RUNAWAY. Only, I know better. And now I have to find my brother.

Seventeen

THE NEXT FEW DAYS ARE A BLUR. The police, who are accustomed to this sort of thing, tell my parents that runaway teenagers generally return within a week, when they get hungry and lonely and tired of sleeping in strange places. Personally, I think it's their excuse to do nothing. "I'll help you, Dylan," Angie says at school the next day. "Just get me a picture of Randy. I'll make flyers on my iMac. We'll post them up around the neighborhood. Someone's bound to have seen him."

So that's what we do. Jonathan and Jake help out, and when we've finished the job, Randy's face is plastered on telephone poles across Bay Ridge, Dyker Heights, and Bensonhurst. In the meantime, my parents cruise the streets in my father's Volvo looking for Randy while Moser, Headbone, and Chloe go around the neighborhood on foot. Nick continues to make calls from his house, but so far, no one has seen or heard from my brother. When I wake up the next morning, there is this brief moment when I don't remember Randy's gone, but soon enough, everything turns black.

Saturday night, Angie begs me to come to a movie with her. "You've done everything you can, Dylan. It's up to Randy now. Please, let's go out. It'll take your mind off things, at least for a while."

We argue back and forth, and finally I give in. We go to see this artsy movie starring that nerdy dude from *Napoleon Dynamite*. I know Angie's chosen the flick because she thinks I'll like it, which I normally would, but tonight the whole thing seems pointless. I can't even follow the story line.

No one's around when I get home. There's a note from my dad saying that he and my mother went out for dinner. *It's funny, I think as I lie on my bed, just a week ago Randy and I were together, right here, shooting the breeze, playing that game we used to play when we were kids.* And then, a minute later, it hits me. Our handshake. Randy's promise. I look at the clock. It's 10 p.m. There's still time.

I grab a jacket and race out the door. I run to the train station and hop the R. When I change for the D, the subway is surprisingly crowded, but soon I realize, *Of course it is.* This is New York City. The Big Apple. And right now there's a jam session going on at Sixth and Waverly. Inside the student lounge at NYU. My brother is there. I know it. He always keeps his word.

When I arrive, I see Randy on the makeshift stage.

Someone has loaned him an electric guitar and he's showing the crowd what he can do. Surrounding him are a half dozen other musicians. A girl with spiky hair and a nose ring is plucking a bass, a guy in a suit and tie is blowing out notes on a harmonica, and a strikingly tall Asian girl in a miniskirt and black boots is banging out a rhythm on drums. Paul, coolest dude in the universe, is moving his magic fingers up and down his sax.

Right now they're doing one of Springsteen's old tunes from *Greetings from Asbury Park, N.J.*, "Spirit in the Night," and the guy on vocals sounds just like the Boss. Paul and Randy and the harmonica player take turns on lead. The audience is really into it. When Randy finally sees me he nods, and when the song is finished he leans over and whispers something to Paul. Paul looks around and spots me in the crowd. He smiles wide and holds up an acoustic guitar—the same one I played with him in Washington Square Park. "And now," he announces into the mike, "please welcome Mr. Dylan Fontaine."

The crowd begins to clap. I'm so jazzed, I forget the fact that I want to wring Randy's neck for leaving home. For scaring the crap out of me for the past several days. I go up there, and together we perform "Little Wing." Paul and Randy swap off on lead, and the notes float smoothly while I strum the rhythm. I don't know if I've ever had a better time playing a piece of music.

When we're done, Paul sets down his sax. "Dylan, hey." We shake hands. "I'm glad you finally showed up, man. Randy said you'd definitely be here, but I was getting worried. Anyway, as you can see, we've been having a great time. You were right about your brother." He jabs his thumb in Randy's direction. "He's the best lead guitarist I've heard in a long time."

"Aw, come on," Randy says. He smiles shyly, but you can tell he's grateful for the compliment. "Anyone would sound good playing with you on sax. Thanks for that song, man. It's one of my favorites."

Paul winks at me. "Yeah, I kind of guessed that." Randy lifts the guitar strap from his shoulder and hands the instrument to Paul. "I'm going to take a short break, all right? I need to talk to my brother." Paul nods, and as the musicians start up another song, Randy and I walk outside into the cool night air.

Now, away from the magic of the jam session, I'm angry all over again. In fact, I'm furious. I throw up my hands. I want to throttle him. "What were you thinking, Randy? Why didn't you call me? Damn it, we've been looking all over for you. Hanging up posters and everything. The police have you on file as a runaway. And you should see your friends—they're going nuts. Chloe's a mess. Mom and Dad are freaking out!"

A little smile plays at the corners of his mouth. He seems to be enjoying the fact that he's been missed. "Really? Wow. Sorry, Dylan, I—"

"Sorry? You're not sorry. Look at you!"

He starts to laugh, and I seriously want to kill him. "Dude, I *am*," he says pleadingly. "You gotta believe me. It's just, well, I didn't realize you'd be so upset. I figured you'd know I needed some time to think. After what happened. I figured everyone would."

"Time to *think?*" I reach out and give him a hard shove. He stumbles back. "You could have been dead for all I knew. Where *were* you?"

"Chill out, Dyl. I was in Queens. Nick has a cousin there—Mike Hewitt. Mike made a few calls and let me know everything was cool at home. I asked him not to tell anyone where I was staying."

"You *asshole!*" I scream. "God, don't you ever think of anyone besides yourself?" I turn away, breathing hard. I'm about to run, but Randy grabs my arm.

"Dylan, hey, come on. Please." He pulls me toward him. I struggle at first, but he's stronger than me. Finally I give in. He hugs me tight to his chest. He smells like leather, smoke, and sweat. I can't help it. I break down and start to cry. "You're right," he says. "You're absolutely right. I should have called you, Dyl. I should have let you know I was safe. But listen, everything's okay, right? You're not in any trouble because of me, are you? Right now, that's all that matters."

"No." I'm slobbering all over his shoulder now. "I dumped the weed in the bay. No one saw me. But the cops came to our house with dogs, just like Chloe said. They didn't find anything."

"You didn't have to do that, Dylan. You didn't have to bail me out."

"Yeah, I know." I take a step back and look him in the eye. "Randy, Nick didn't rat on you. He admitted to hiding the weed at our house, but he said it was there for just a day or two, until he could move it somewhere else. It was a jack-ass move on his part—he said he needed the money for the tour, for the van—but he didn't mean you any harm. It was Franz—the cops were on to him, so he gave them your names."

Randy sighs. "Franz. Yeah, I guess that's no surprise. Thanks for telling me. Sorry to get you in the middle of it."

"Nick's on house arrest," I say. "The cops found some weed in his room, but not enough to press distribution charges."

Randy nods. "Yeah, his cousin told me." After a minute he gives me a wry smile. "So it looks like the Dead Musicians Society won't be going on that tour after all. I suppose it's just as well. The Sewer Rats *suck.*"

I manage to laugh a little. "You got that right." It's my turn to grab my brother and hug him tight. "Thank God I found you. I felt like it was my fault, you know, for blaming Nick. I figured that's why you ran."

"Hey, nothing's your fault. You were just doing your job." He smiles a little. "Looking out for me. Now, come on, let's go back in and play some music."

After a few more songs, I look at the time. It's almost 1 a.m. I'd love to stay, but I know my parents are probably worried. "We should go," I say to Randy.

"Listen, Dylan," he says. "I'm not ready yet. I still need a couple more days to sort things out. Paul said I could crash at his place. Just tell Mom and Dad I'm all right, and I'll be back soon, okay?"

I don't like the sound of this arrangement, but by the

look on Randy's face I can tell he's not going to budge. I hold out my hand. "That's a promise, right, dude? You won't bag on me?"

He grips my hand tight. "You got my word."

When I make it home, my parents are in the living room, anxiously awaiting my return. "Dylan! Thank God!" My mother jumps up and runs to me. Without even thinking, I wrap my arms around her.

"Randy's okay," I say. I look at my dad, sitting on the couch. He closes his eyes and breathes a sigh of relief. "I was with him, just now, in the city," I go on. "He'll be home in a few days." I expect my father to start ranting about asinine teenagers, barraging me with a million questions about why Randy left in the first place, but instead he gets up and puts his arms around both my mother and me. The hug feels clumsy and awkward, but good at the same time.

The following morning I wake up to Tripod meowing his head off. I figure he's gotten himself locked in my mom's studio again, but when I open the door I find my mother sitting in the middle of the floor surrounded by cardboard boxes. Tripod is perched on one, screeching his dissatisfaction. Already she's packed her computer, her books, the Japanese chest where she keeps her paintbrushes. In the far corner is the easel where her pastel portrait once sat, folded up and ready to go. "Hey," she says, attempting a smile.

I'm not sure what I've been expecting. After all the time my parents spent together searching for Randy, I thought maybe there was a chance my mom might stay. I guess I was wrong.

I don't say anything. I close the door and go back to my room. I search through my vintage LPs and finally choose *Led Zeppelin II*. The chaos of the music matches my mood. As Robert Plant belts out "Ramble On," there's a knock on my door. "Dylan, may I come in?" When I don't answer, my mom enters, lifts the needle, and sits beside me.

The room is deathly quiet now. There was a time when my mom and I could talk easily about ordinary, everyday things, but that time is past. "So you're leaving again," I say.

"Yes, honey, I am."

I nod, and there's a long stretch of silence. "Dylan," my mom finally says, "I want to thank you for stopping by the studio last week. It meant a lot to me. And I'd like to explain something. I painted those pictures because they're happy memories. I didn't mean to upset you."

I stare out the window. A blue jay flies by with a piece of straw in its beak. It's building a nest. A home.

"I know this is hard for you to accept, Dylan, and I wish it didn't have to be this way, but when I was here, living in this house with your dad constantly gone, I felt so alone. When he was home, it seems like all we did was argue. Where I am now, it's . . . where I need to be. I have friends, people who care, my art. It's a community."

The words sting. What am I supposed to say? *Gee, Mom, I'm so happy for you? So glad you found people who care?* But the truth is, I'd known for a while that my mother was unhappy. I just didn't want to admit it.

"I still love your dad," she says. "I always will. He's a good father to you and Randy. But the two of us together . . . it doesn't work anymore. I tried for a long time. In a way, he's married to his job."

I think back to when Randy and I were young, when my dad was still a resident at the hospital, before he got his own practice. Things were different—sure, he worked a lot, but he was there for us and for my mother, too. I guess I understand why she painted those pictures. She wanted to remember the good times.

My mom reaches into her pocket and pulls out a piece of paper. "This is my new address. While I was in Paris an apartment opened near Philippe's place in the Village. I'm taking it. It's got an extra bedroom and, well, I'd really love if you'd come stay with me on the weekends, or whenever you can. Randy, too."

She hands me the paper. I stare at the address. None of this makes sense. "But . . . I don't get it. I thought you and Philippe were together."

She gives me a strange look. "Oh . . . no, honey. We're friends. Good friends. I thought you knew that. He was helping me out until I could find a place of my own."

"Oh." For some reason this makes me feel even worse. My mom's not leaving us for someone else—she's just . . . leaving. "Does Dad know that?" I ask.

"Of course. Why? He didn't lead you to believe something else, did he?"

I think for a moment. My dad never came out and said my mom was having an affair with Philippe, but then again, he never said she *wasn't*. "Um, no, he didn't," I say. "I guess . . . it was my mistake."

She shakes her head. "Wow, all this time you thought . . . Randy, too? Well, that explains a lot. I'm sorry, Dylan. I wish I'd known. I would have cleared it up right away." Tentatively, she reaches over and takes my hand. "Anyway, I hope you'll come and stay with me. You don't have to answer right now, just think about it, okay? And maybe you can talk to Randy when he comes home? He won't speak to me at all."

I stuff the paper into my back pocket. "Okay, Mom. I'll think about it. I'll talk to Randy, too."

"Thank you." She smiles and gives my hand a squeeze. "Dylan? I saw the sketch of the girl hanging in the studio." For a moment I think she's mistaken the drawing for Randy's, the same way Nick did. But I'm wrong. "It's beautiful," she says. "Your best piece yet. I was wondering if I might take it with me, to hang in my new place. I know it's asking a lot, but I really love the piece."

I look at my mom. Her eyes are hopeful. "Yeah, sure," I say. "I drew several of those, so it's no problem. I . . . want you to have it."

"Thank you, Dylan." We sit there together for a while, and when Tripod begins to screech again, my mother returns to the messy business of packing.

Later, after I've had time to think, I find my dad. He's in the family room watching TV. It's Sunday, so as long as none of his patients go into labor, he's got the day off. When I walk in, he pats the seat next to him. "You want to watch the game with me, Dylan? The Giants are leading fourteen to seven and—"

"No, Dad. I need to ask you a question. An important one."

"All right." He turns down the volume. "What is it?"

"I talked to Mom. She explained to me that she and Philippe are just friends. Nothing more. I know you never came out and said they were having an affair, but you also never said they weren't. This whole time, Randy and I thought she left you—left *us*—for him. Why didn't you tell us the truth? Why did you let us believe that?"

At first my dad looks stunned; then he looks ashamed. He lowers his head and sighs deeply. "I never meant to lie to you, Dylan. Or to Randy. But when your mom first left, I was so upset, so angry, and I guess it was easier that way. To let her take the blame. It was wrong. I should have told you and Randy the truth."

"Yeah, you should have." I stare at my dad for a while. His head's still down, his shoulders slumped. What he did was wrong, so I guess the question is: will I forgive him? Slowly I walk over and take a seat beside him. Maybe he hasn't been around much lately, but he's here now. That counts for something. I put a hand on his shoulder. "It's okay, Dad. Don't beat yourself up. I understand. Really. What do you say we watch the rest of the game together?"

So that's what we do. Until the phone rings and he gets called in for a delivery. It's a quick one—he's home by five—

and when he walks through the door he's carrying an armful of groceries. He gives Vanya the night off and asks my mother to stay for dinner. She agrees. To my surprise, he whips up this really great-smelling gourmet meal. Shrimp scampi with asparagus and pine nuts. He even breaks out an expensive bottle of wine and pours us each a glass.

"Before we begin, I have an announcement to make," he says. He glances sadly at Randy's empty chair. "I wish Randy was here too, but at least for now we know he's safe. Anyway"—he lifts his cup in a toast—"I've hired a new partner. A young, well-respected doctor from Columbia Medical Center. He'll be starting in a couple of weeks."

My mom looks stunned, but then she smiles at my father and lifts her glass. "That's wonderful, Paul. I'm happy for you. For your new partner, too. He's a lucky man."

When I get over my shock, I chime in, "That's great, Dad. So does that mean . . . ?" I'm about to say, *no more housekeeper?* But I don't. It's hard to admit, but I kind of like having Vanya around. Instead, I say, ". . . we can watch the playoffs together?"

"I think that can be arranged."

We clink glasses, and before my mother takes a sip of her wine, she smiles at my dad and mouths, *Thank you.*

Eighteen

RANDY KEEPS HIS WORD. He arrives in Brooklyn the following evening, but not in the way I expect. At 11 p.m., as I'm getting ready for bed, the phone rings. When I pick up, the person on the other end barks, "This is officer Greenwood calling from the Sixty-eighth Precinct police station. Is Dr. Fontaine home?"

Greenwood. I cringe, remembering the way the dude so mercilessly slapped those handcuffs around my wrists outside Century 21. I can picture him now, scowling, grinding his teeth, sipping his poisoned coffee, untwisting the lid of the urine sample container. "Um . . . no," I say. "My father got called in for a delivery at the hospital. Can I . . . take a message?"

"Yeah. Tell him we found his missing son. Picked him up in the neighborhood, along with a few of his buddies. They're all being charged with POM. Possession of marijuana. Your father's going to have to come here to bail him out. Otherwise he'll spend the night in jail."

"Oh, okay," I say. "I'll let him know. Thank you, sir. Thanks for finding him."

"Yeah, sure thing, kid." He hangs up.

Quickly I dial the hospital. It turns out my father is in the operating room performing an emergency C-section. I leave a message with the nurse at the desk. "Please tell my father I'll meet him at the police station," I say. Next I hang up and dial a car service. To be perfectly honest, I'm going to the Sixty-eighth Precinct police station for two reasons. One, to offer Randy moral support, and two, to see the imbeciles behind bars. It took a while, but finally, justice is served.

"Well, well, look who it is," Greenwood says when I arrive. He's sitting at his desk, shuffling through a stack of paperwork. Officer Burns is in another room, talking to a guy with a huge bandage on his head. "Mr. Fruit of the Loom. Mr. . . . what was that again? Oh, yeah, Mr. Trans Fat. How's it going?"

"Fine," I say. "Just fine." Chloe is sitting on a stool in the hallway outside the holding cell. She waves to me. "Um, Officer Greenwood?" I say. "My dad will be here as soon as he can. I'd like to stay with my brother until he arrives."

He rolls his eyes. "Jeez, what's your brother doing, inviting his whole fan club? This isn't Grand Central Station, kid. And I ain't no babysitter."

"Yes, sir, I know, but I won't cause any trouble. I promise."

"Oh, right. I forgot. It's the *polite* juvenile delinquent. All right, fine, whatever."

After Greenwood frisks me to make sure I'm not carrying a dangerous weapon, I walk over to the cell. Moser is sprawled out on the concrete bench reading *Memoirs of a Pervert* on the wall, while Headbone stares at the STD-infested toilet. Randy is pressed up against the bars, holding Chloe's hand. "Hey, Dyl," he says. "Glad you could make it."

Chloe turns to me and grins. "So the dopeheads finally got what was coming to them, hey, Dylan?"

"Dylan!" Headbone bolts over, grasping the iron bars. "Dude, you got to get us out of here! That cop Greenwood called my parents and they actually told him to leave me here overnight. Moser's did the same thing. They said it'll teach us a lesson, whatever that means. Can you believe it? And now"—he lowers his voice and looks around—"I'm trying to flush the weed out of my system, you know, before the piss test, and the dude won't even give me another glass of water. I mean, what is this, a fascist country? Oh, and the other guy, Officer Burns, when he found out that your father was the almighty Vagina Head, he whipped out his wallet and started showing us pictures of his kid. The one your father delivered. Like we really care at a time like this!"

"Oh, I don't know," Moser says, finally peeling his eyes away from the wall. "I thought Burns's kid was kind of cute."

Headbone throws up his hands. "Dylan, dude, I'm surrounded by incompetents! You got to help me, man!"

"Sure, Headbone," I say. "I'll help you. I'll sit here and keep you company for a while." I grin and take a seat next to Chloe. By far, this is the best show in town.

When my father arrives about an hour later, he races to the cell. "Thanks for calling, Dylan. Randy, are you all right?"

"Yeah, Dad, I'm fine. Listen, I'm . . . sorry about all this. I shouldn't have—"

My dad holds up a hand. "We'll talk about it later. I'm just glad you're safe. Right now we need to get you out of here. I'll speak to the officers."

"Dad? Um, hey . . . if it's all right with you, I'd like to stay here for the night. Moser's and Headbone's parents aren't coming, so the guys could use the company."

"Oh?" My dad looks around, surprised. Headbone and Moser hang their heads sheepishly.

"I'll keep an eye on them, Dr. Fontaine," Chloe says. "Why don't you go home and get a good night's sleep? I'll call you if there's a problem."

My dad hems and haws for a while and finally gives in. "Well . . . okay. If that's what you prefer."

Burns and Greenwood are waiting to talk to my father now, but before we leave, Randy holds out his hand. "Thanks for coming, Dad."

My dad pauses, looks at Randy, and takes his hand. Without a word, they shake. "Sure thing," my dad says. "We'll talk tomorrow, okay?"

Burns and Greenwood and the judge at the courthouse are pretty tough on Randy, Headbone, and Moser. As expected, all three test positive for marijuana, and to atone for their crime they are each sentenced to a three-month class on the evils of substance abuse, along with a three-hundred-dollar fine, forty hours of community service, and drug testing to be done sporadically by a police officer at McKinley High. Nick, it turns out, will share his bandmates' fate once he's off house arrest.

About a week after their court date, I come home from school and hear Randy playing a new song on his guitar. I head to the basement. Chloe is singing lyrics I've never heard before while Headbone drums out a beat and Moser plays a bass line. It's rough, but it sounds pretty good. I listen for a few minutes, then go upstairs. As I'm whipping up a soy protein shake, Chloe joins me in the kitchen. "So what do you think?"

"It's good," I say. "I like it."

She grins, pulls up a stool, and sits at the counter. "Randy and I have been talking. He wants to stop doing covers for parties—refocus the band, get some original songs together. If we work hard, we'll eventually be able to record a demo, pass it around to clubs, maybe get some gigs."

"That's great," I say. "Honestly, it's about time."

I pour part of my shake into a glass for Chloe. She takes a sip. "And the best part is Randy told me he would stay clean. Even *after* the drug testing. He's going to talk to the guys. Nick, too. Finally, Randy's getting serious about his music."

We finish the shake and go downstairs. Randy tosses me his old acoustic and says, "Come on, Dylan, play with us for a while. Show these guys how it's done."

✳ ✳ ✳

Meanwhile, the screening of *The Latent Powers of Dylan Fontaine* is drawing near. Angie and Jonathan have finished their edits and now Angie is busily working on promotion. She's printed up invitations and I've agreed to help pass them out. On my way to art class Monday morning I see Val Knudsen standing in the hallway, gazing at something on the wall. I dig in my pocket and pull out an invitation. "Hey, Fontaine," she says. "Come here. Get a load of this."

To my surprise, taped to the wall is my portrait of Val—the one with the ghosted-in background of a girl holding the Chinese symbols for life and death—and beside it is her drawing of me. At least, that's what I think it is. "Looks like Wiseman liked our portraits," she says. "They're the only two he chose to display."

"Um," I say, pointing to the wall. "Is that . . . *me?*"

She grins and gives me a shove. "Yeah, of course it is, Fontaine. Can't you tell?"

"Well . . ." All I can say is that Val has made last year's portrait of Mary Flannery—the one with the knife in her throat and one bloody eyeball hanging from its socket—look tame. Staring back at me is an AC/DC death demon with hissing snakes for teeth and a lightning bolt shooting through its skull.

"It's got your look of surprise, don't you think?" Val says.

I study the drawing a little more closely. Strangely, there *is* something that reminds me of myself. "Yeah, yeah, actually, I see what you mean."

"Anyway, Fontaine, I like the way you drew me." She gazes at the wall. "You captured my essence, you know?"

I shrug. "That's what I was trying for. Oh, here," I say, handing her the invitation. "Will you come?"

She looks at the paper and a smile spreads across her face. "You better believe I'll be there, Fontaine. A short film starring *you*? I wouldn't miss it."

On the night of the screening, the auditorium at NYU is packed. A total of fifteen films will be shown, and by the luck of the draw, Angie's is last. Jonathan and I take seats on either side of Angie, and I look around. Everyone we've invited is here. When the lights dim and the first film begins, Angie takes hold of my hand and Jonathan's. Right away I can see that the competition is fierce. Each film is well crafted, visually appealing, and unique. The students have done their homework.

Finally the announcer says, "Now we are pleased to present *The Latent Powers of Dylan Fontaine*, by Angie McCarthy." Angie's been very secretive about her editing, so I'm not sure what to expect. As the film begins I discover that she's made a series of short action clips, and interspersed between them are interviews from that memorable night at the Beanery. I watch with wonder and horror as Toulouse-Lautrec announces, "Come on now, cats! Don't leave this man hanging! Surely there's someone out there who wants to cover my friend Bony Ass!" I laugh when I see my face as Taz falls to the subway floor after a fatal blow from the imaginary Mike Tyson. I feel the heat of the torches and the buzzing of the chain saws as the Aussie juggles them, one by one, over my head.

After a while, everything becomes clear. *The Latent Powers of Dylan Fontaine* is a story about an ordinary dude, me, taking a few chances, finding humor in the world, discovering who he is. And as I glance around I can tell the audience is really into it. Halfway through, I turn to Angie. "Everyone likes it," I whisper. She smiles and squeezes my hand more tightly. Suddenly, I realize that Angie's not only made the movie for herself, for this screening, for the possible win; she's made it for me.

In the final scene I'm near the fountain at Washington Square Park. Loose Marbles is playing and I pull Angie into the dance circle. "Hey, wait a minute," I say, leaning over in my chair. "You told me this wasn't going to be in the film. You said—"

"Shhh, quiet, Dylan. I changed my mind, all right? Just watch."

The tattooed girl sings *"Send me to the 'lectric chair"* while Angie and I begin to slow-dance. Next is our disastrous kiss. I can barely watch. Before I press my mouth to Angie's, I notice a faint smile on her lips. She closes her eyes and kisses me back. I brace myself for the next part—Angie pushing me away—but suddenly the movie ends. To my surprise, she's cut it right there. The audience cheers. I could be wrong, but I think they're cheering for *me*. Dylan Fontaine, the hero of the story, finally found the courage to go after the girl.

I glance at Jonathan. He nods and whispers, "It's time, Dylan. 'All the world's a stage, and all the men and women merely players.' "

I'm not sure what he means at first, but soon I realize what I have to do. I stand up and pull Angie to her feet. The crowd cheers more loudly. And then I do it. I kiss her right in front of everyone. This time she doesn't push me away. She wraps her arms around my neck and doesn't let go.

From the audience, Headbone calls out, "Dylan! Studmeister! Give us lessons!"

Acknowledgments

I'd like to thank my friends and members of my critique group: Varian Johnson, Julie Lake, Brian Yansky, and Frances Hill Yansky; my agent, Laura Rennert; my talented editor, Françoise Bui, who loved Dylan from the start; and my husband, Ed, who laughed at all the funny parts.

About the Author

April Lurie is a native New Yorker. She is the author of *Brothers, Boyfriends & Other Criminal Minds* and *Dancing in the Streets of Brooklyn*. She lives near Austin, Texas, with her husband and their four children. Visit her at www.aprillurie.com.